The Payback Adventure

The Billionaires of Silicon Forest

Billionaire Matchmaker, Book 2

MELISSA MCCLONE

The Payback Adventure: The Billionaires of Silicon Forest
Billionaire Matchmaker (Book 2)
Copyright © 2024 Melissa McClone
Second Edition

Original version published as
The Billionaire's Wedding Masquerade.

ALL RIGHTS RESERVED

The unauthorized reproduction or distribution of this copyrighted work, in any form by any electronic, mechanical, or other means, is illegal and forbidden, without written permission of the author, except in the case of brief quotations embodied in critical articles and reviews.

This is a work of fiction. Characters, settings, names, and occurrences are products of the author's imagination or used fictitiously and bear no resemblance to any actual person, living or dead, places or settings and/or occurrences. Any incidences of resemblance are purely coincidental.

Cover by Elizabeth Mackey

Cardinal Press, LLC
February 2024
ISBN-13: 9781944777890

Dedication

For everyone who wanted Henry's story
and Amy, Betsy, Shirley, and Virginia.

Thanks to Brent and Vanessa at LaFollettes Berry Farm,
Jenny Andersen, Dr. Terry Sedgewick, and Dave Working
for answering my questions.
Any mistakes are mine.

Note From The Author

I'm so excited to finally bring you Henry Davenport's story. He's one of my favorite secondary characters and showed up in so many of my books through three series. *A Payback Adventure* is part of an interconnected series, but it is a standalone romance. Some of his previous matchmaking couples do appear in this story. If you're curious about what the billionaire matchmaker's efforts have accomplished, here's the list:

- Brett and Laurel in *The Wedding Lullaby* (One Night to Forever, book 1)
- Ryland and Brynn in *Love on the Slopes* (One Night to Forever, book 4)
- Blaise and Hadley in *The Wife Finder* (Billionaires of Silicon Forest, book 1)
- Wes and Paige in *The Wish Maker* (Billionaires of Silicon Forest, book 2)
- Dash and Iris in *The Deal Breaker* (Billionaires of Silicon Forest, book 3)
- Adam and Cambria in *The Gold Digger* (Billionaires of Silicon Forest, prequel 1)
- Kieran and Selah in *The Kiss Catcher* (Billionaires of Silicon Forest, prequel 2)
- Mason and Rachael in *The Game Changer* (Billionaires of Silicon Forest, prequel 3)
- Cade and Cynthia in *The Island Adventure* (Billionaire Matchmaker, book 1)

And there are at least two more books in his Billionaire Matchmaker series after this one, so Henry's not quite done yet!

Enjoy,
Melissa

Prologue

September

Just call me the billionaire cupid!

With anticipation thrumming in his veins, Henry Davenport pushed open the door to the labor and delivery suite with his shoulder. One hand carried a bouquet and the other a teddy bear. He'd been awake for more than thirty-six hours. Dash Cabot had texted their group chat that Iris's water had broken at ten last night, and sleep wouldn't come. Henry knew it wouldn't until his newest godchild had arrived safely.

Not that he was tired.

He'd been waiting for this moment since Iris and Dash announced her pregnancy at Henry's birthday party in Hawaii on April Fools' Day. It had been the best present on record. Second only to Cade Armstrong Waters proposing to Cynthia

Sterling after the island adventure Henry had sent them on as part of his birthday celebration. That had been the last time he'd played matchmaker, but he didn't do it with everyone. No, he made sure the couple belonged together.

Like Dash and Iris Cabot.

And now they'd even had their child on a holiday—Labor Day. How fitting was that?

Henry entered the room quietly, keeping his steps soft in case anyone was sleeping. It had been a long night and an even longer day for the couple, and though Dash had texted him that it was okay for a visit, Henry wanted to be mindful of what they'd all been through. Something he'd learned after the birth of Noelle Matthews, his goddaughter.

The sight of Dash holding his newborn and staring at a sleeping Iris stopped Henry in his tracks. They were a family in every sense of the word. Dash smiled softly and wiped his eyes.

Henry's heart stilled. The love flowing from husband to wife was almost palpable. His vision blurred, and he blinked, refocusing on the hospital bed.

I knew they belonged together.

He'd known the way he had with so many others. Henry had a gift for matchmaking that would continue to benefit his friends, even though they all told him to stop.

But Henry had no intention of stopping. That wouldn't be fair to the other couples who needed him to push—though shove might be a more apt description—them together the way Dash Cabot had required him to open his eyes to the perfect woman, who happened to be his best friend.

"Congratulations." Henry approached the new family. "Being a dad suits you."

"Dad." Dash stared at the baby. "I like the sound of that. What do you think, son?"

Iris and Dash had kept the gender a secret during the pregnancy. Henry set the flowers on the bed tray but held on to the stuffed animal. "You had a boy."

Dash nodded.

Iris didn't stir. "She must be tired."

"Exhausted and taking a well-deserved nap." Dash smiled at his wife. "I've always been so amazed by her, but the way she gave birth to our son… Incredible.

"Meet Brecken Henry Cabot."

Henry nearly fell over. "You—"

"You *are* his godfather."

His vision blurred once again. "I am."

"Brecken, this is your uncle Henry."

He showed the baby the teddy bear, not that a newborn could focus on anything except the color. Then he set the stuffed animal on the bed to take a closer look at the baby swaddled in a blanket and wearing a pink-and-blue striped cap. "He's handsome like me."

Dash laughed. "Iris said you'd say that. Would you like to hold him?"

"Please. Let me wash my hands." Henry did that quickly in the nearby sink and returned to the bedside. He carefully took the baby from Dash, making sure to support Brecken's head. "He's perfect. Oh, you and your uncle Henry will have great fun together. I promise you that."

"Thank you."

Henry glanced at Dash. "For what?"

"For my family. Without you, I'd probably still be a workaholic staying up and playing video games on the weekends, missing Iris after she quit."

"You've come a long way, Master Dashiell." Dash was the youngest of the Billionaires of Silicon Forest. He was the smartest of the group but had few social skills, especially when it came to women. "And you're lucky Iris loves you so much. Not many women would have put up with what you did."

Dash hung his head and reached out to stroke Iris's hair. "Don't I know it, but I've tried to make it up to her since then, and I'll keep trying. I love her so much."

"I know you do. That's why I couldn't give up on you, either." Henry cuddled Brecken closer. Thank goodness Henry hadn't. Now, he had two godchildren, and he wanted more.

Who would he play matchmaker with next?

Chapter One

"What are you smiling about, Henry?" Cade Armstrong Waters, an attorney turned child advocate, sat across from him in the red vinyl booth. "Hole-in-the-wall cafés are more my style than yours."

Henry Davenport stared at the nubile blond server. "Not with her working here."

"She's attractive, but a little young for my tastes," Cade said. "Age has never stopped you before."

It hadn't. Henry had gone out with younger women, but lately he'd dated closer to his age or older women. Still, he wanted her. Take away the pink knee-length skirt, the white shirt, the stained apron, the ugly white shoes, and the nude-colored support hose not even Mrs. Zimmer, his middle-aged housekeeper, would be caught dead wearing, and she'd be perfect. Barely dressed, which would make her all the more perfect.

He grinned at the thought. Perhaps it was too much to imagine she wore short skirts and stilettos when she wasn't at work, but hey, this was his daydream, and the server had to spend her tips on something. What better than sexy clothes and shoes?

"Thank you, Cynthia, for suggesting we stop here," Henry said. "I'm certain the food will be delicious. The view is *tres magnifique.*"

"I only wanted to eat before we went wine tasting." Cade's bride-to-be, Cynthia Sterling, pursed her glossed lips. "Do you plan on asking her out?"

"Why not?" Henry asked. "I've dated actresses, models, dancers, and socialites. Even you, darling."

"Only once. Thank goodness."

Cade placed a protective arm around his fiancée. "Lucky for me, the two of you were more like brother and sister than boyfriend and girlfriend."

She leaned against him. "Lucky for me, I met you." The tenderness of Cynthia's smile touched Henry's heart. Once again, his matchmaking skills had been perfect. No fine-tuning or adjustment needed. Henry truly enjoyed few things, but seeing his friends find true love was at the top of the list. And no one could argue with his success.

He thought about the birth of his godchild Brecken last month and grinned.

"Well, it's not like Henry's interested in having a relationship with any woman," Cynthia added.

Henry nodded. "Everyone knows I don't do relation-ships."

"You could always hire her." Cade raised a brow. "Have her wear one of those little black French maid outfits and help out your housekeeper."

Henry grinned at the image forming in his mind. "I like that idea."

Cynthia rolled her eyes. "You'd probably want her to carry one of those feather dusters."

Cade laughed and patted Cynthia's hand. As her engagement ring sparkled, Henry noticed her French manicure. "Your fingernails have grown back nicely."

"Finally," Cynthia said, flexing her fingers. "After your deserted-island adventure, I thought my hands would never look the same. Though I still have a few calluses."

Cade kissed the top of her hand. "Just a reminder of what we had to go through to find each other."

Henry grinned. "A small price to pay for happily ever after."

"A small price?" Cynthia frowned. "I ended up with a bamboo pole stuck in my foot and had surgery."

"I'm sorry about your foot." Henry had covered her medical bills and still sent her a bouquet each week to make up for her injury. "But that was a freak accident. No one else has ever gotten hurt."

"Accidents do happen, I suppose." Cynthia narrowed her eyes. "Who knows what will happen during your next birthday adventure?"

"Two people will fall in love." Henry rubbed his palms together. "Just like you did. And Brett and Laurel Matthews, too. Not to mention all the other happy couples, now that I no longer limit my matchmaking prowess to my birthday."

She shook her head. "We know."

He laughed. "Admit it, darling. I've become an accomplished matchmaker."

"You've let success go to your head." Cynthia sighed. "Next you'll want us to call you Cupid."

"That has a nice ring," he admitted. "But Henry will do."

Cynthia leaned forward. "You know, Henry, it isn't right to play around with people's lives this way."

"It is right, darling." Henry flashed her his most dazzling smile. Of course, she was immune to the effect, but perhaps the server caught a glimpse. He loved flirting and the nuances that went with it. "In fact, matchmaking is my duty to those I care most about. If not for me, you wouldn't be engaged."

Cade nodded. "He's got a point, Sterling."

"I'm grateful to you for introducing me to Cade, but there has to be another way to find love than having you play puppet master." She spoke with tenderness, and Henry knew she wasn't trying to offend him. "Someone could get hurt. Not just an injured foot but a broken heart. Or worse."

Henry drew back. "Don't tell me you want me to stop!"

"I won't tell you," Cynthia said. "But I do."

Little Noelle and Brecken popped into his head. He loved his godchildren so much. Besides… "My friends would be too disappointed if I stopped."

"Not all your friends," Cade admitted. "You do enough for your friends by planning trips and parties and all sorts of other fun things. The matchmaking isn't necessary."

Cynthia nodded. "Neither are your adventures."

"Both are very necessary," Henry countered, feeling defensive. "I'm not stopping."

"It's time you entered the real world, Henry," Cynthia said. "If you knew what being sent on an adventure was like, you would change your tune."

"I would love to be sent on an adventure."

"You would?" Cynthia asked.

"Be careful how you answer," Cade cautioned.

"Of course. It would be fun," Henry said without any hesitation. No one would ever go to the effort to create an adventure for him. It was too much work. No one had that kind of free time or money. Not the way he did.

Cynthia straightened. "I'm so happy to hear you say that."

The beautiful young server stepped from the kitchen and walked his way. The sway of her hips hypnotized him. He focused on her heart-shaped face. A pair of blue eyes met his. Clear and bright, her gaze made Henry straighten.

"Welcome to the Berry Bistro." She greeted him with a wide smile, and he sucked in a breath. "I'm Elisabeth. May I take your order?"

Her soft voice was perfect for whispering sweet and not-so-sweet words into his ear. "Do you have any specials that could possibly compare to your dazzling smile, Lizzie?"

He expected her to flirt back. Women always did with him.

Instead, she pressed her lips together. "No specials this morning, and it's Elisabeth with an *S*."

Not just a pretty face. Charm alone was not going to win her over. He liked that. Most women simply fell at his feet. And wallet. "My mistake, Elisabeth with an *S*."

She readied her pencil. "Your order?"

The only thing Henry wanted was her. Nothing else mattered at that moment. Not food, water, oxygen—strike that. He never gave up oxygen. The powerful urge to win her over took him aback. It must be the challenge he found so appealing.

"Would you like to order?" Elisabeth asked again.

"Give us a minute, please," Cade said.

"I'd love some bottled water," Cynthia said. "Do you have Pellegrino?"

Elisabeth bit her lower lip as if to keep herself from making a sassy reply. "I'm sorry, we don't."

"That's okay," Cynthia said with a reassuring tone. "Just bring whatever you have and lemon wedges, too."

As Elisabeth walked away, Henry felt an urge to follow her, even if it meant stepping into what was no doubt a greasy, smelly kitchen. He leaned back against the booth.

A challenge was one thing. This was…different.

The strength of his attraction took him by surprise. Lately, it seemed to take something extravagant or someone larger than life to work up his interest. Not that anything appealed to him for long.

Cynthia stared at him. "She doesn't seem like your usual type."

"Nothing wrong with a natural, girl-next-door type," Cade replied before Henry had the chance.

The words earned him a good-hearted elbow from Cynthia. "I'm the only natural girl for you."

"Of course you are," Cade said. "But a man can look."

And I'm enjoying the view, Henry thought.

Elisabeth picked up mason jars used as vases from the

empty tables on her way to the kitchen. She looked like a bride in her crisp white shirt with her hands full of flowers. Henry got a flash of her wearing a wedding gown made from the finest white silk, with a flowing veil held in place by an intricately woven floral wreath and a coordinating bouquet in her hands. He wasn't simply imagining her as any bride. He envisioned Elisabeth as *his* bride.

The tenderness of the image surprised him. The reality of the thought terrified him. He didn't do brides.

Henry shook the thought from his mind. He had no interest in a relationship or anything that inspired thoughts of a bride, especially his. Time to put all this behind him before it got bad.

But bad didn't begin to explain how a server from a blink-and-you'll-miss-it town on the edge of Oregon's Yamhill wine country had left Henry speechless and shaking in his Church's. The only thing left to do was leave. "Let's find another restaurant."

Two small lines formed above Cynthia's nose. "What's wrong with this one?"

"The service," he said without any hesitation.

"I'm the one who asked her to give us a minute," Cade said.

"It can't be Elisabeth," Cynthia added. "You said she was lovely."

"No, I mean, yes, she is lovely. But I didn't say it. Well, I just did, but not before." Henry shifted in his seat. "Can we just go?"

"Well, well, well. This is an interesting turn of events." A smug smile formed on Cynthia's lips. "Of all the women in the world, a server from some Podunk town has finally spooked the world's most confirmed bachelor."

"I'm not spooked." But even as Henry said the words, he knew he was more than spooked and wanted it to stop. Now.

"You're pale," Cade added.

Henry raised his chin. "I'm hungry."

"Then we should stay and eat so we can leave your server a nice big tip." Cynthia smirked.

"She's not my server. And I'm not interested in her."

"I've never seen a woman have an effect on you like this." Mischief gleamed in Cynthia's eyes. "You really like her."

"I like the look of her. I don't know her. And I won't be getting to know her." Henry glanced toward the kitchen and hoped her shift was over. "Elisabeth's a small-town server. I'm a… I'm me. What would we talk about?"

Cade laughed. "You want to talk to her?"

He had a point, but Henry didn't want to think about that. He didn't want to think about the things they could do together. He didn't want to think about her at all.

"I don't want to talk to her," Henry said. "I don't want anything to do with her. Can we go?"

"Oh, knock it off." Cynthia nudged Cade. "Excuse me, honey, I need to powder my nose."

Henry fiddled with his paper napkin as she slid out of the booth. "Elisabeth seems…sweet. Innocent."

"That's never stopped you before," Cynthia said before walking away.

It hadn't. Her comeback made the situation clearer.

The sooner Henry put Elisabeth with an *S* and this two-bit little town behind him, the better.

Chapter Two

Elisabeth's hand trembled as she placed a bottle of water on her tray. She couldn't believe the guy from table four, who looked like a movie star with his expressive hazel-green eyes and killer smile, had been flirting with her. And she couldn't believe she'd shut him down.

Stupid move, but she hadn't been thinking straight. She hadn't been thinking at all.

She should have played along, done all those flirty things she used to know how to do, and gotten a big, fat tip. The trio at table four had money. The expensive shoes were always a giveaway.

Kathy Alexander placed a small plate of lemon wedges on the tray. "Here you go."

"Thanks."

Kathy owned the Berry Bistro, which until two weeks ago

and for the past nineteen years had been called Kathy's Korner Kafé. That was until Berry Patch, Oregon, Elisabeth's hometown, wanted to become upscale to appeal to wine country visitors. Shops and restaurants changed their names and remodeled—or repainted the walls in the case of the bistro—as best as they could. Of course, the bistro was still a corner café. For now. "Is this for table four?"

Elisabeth nodded.

"Those two men are lookers. Especially the guy with the light brown hair and brown eyes."

"Hazel," Elisabeth corrected. "His eyes are hazel."

She hadn't liked being stared at with those eyes. His gaze had been so intense, so intimate. Elisabeth had felt exposed, naked, and wanted to run away.

"He called me Lizzie." She'd been called Beth, Bess, Bessey, Lissie, and Lis. Those names didn't bother her. But Lizzie? "Every time I hear that name, I think of Lizzie Borden chopping up her parents with an ax. It gives me the willies."

"He could call me whatever he wanted, and I'd answer." Kathy sighed. "Sure would like a taste of that eye candy."

"He's too much of a pretty boy."

"I remember when you used to love pretty boys."

And look where that had gotten her.

Elisabeth tightened her grip on the tray. "That was a long time ago."

"Not that long ago, honey." Kathy stared at her. "And that pretty boy at table four looked as if the only thing he wanted to order was you."

"I'm not on the menu."

"Maybe you should be." Kathy's eyes darkened with concern. "Have you found someone to fill in for Manny?"

"No."

Manny Gallegos ran the berry farm for Elisabeth. Between the kids and her serving job, she did what she could with the farm, and Manny did the rest. Or had until he'd had to return to Mexico. And this late in the year, all her regular field hands had also returned home. Normally, she and Manny could handle it together. But alone…

She bit her lip. "I thought he would be back by now, but his mother took a turn for the worse."

"You should fire him."

"I can't." Manny had been her father's trusted foreman, and he'd become both her right- and left-hand person. He'd been the one constant on the farm. Or had been until two weeks ago. But Elisabeth understood what commitment to family meant. "You don't fire someone because their mother is ill. He needs to be with her."

"What about your needs?" Kathy asked.

She needed someone to help her prepare the farm for winter. An extra pair of hands. Someone with two good arms and legs who could follow directions. It was already the beginning of October. Her stomach clenched. "I just need to find some temporary help."

Temporary, cheap help.

"Where?" Kathy asked. "And how will you pay them since you kept Manny on salary?"

Elisabeth could do the work alone, but she'd have to quit this job. And berry farming alone wouldn't support her family. She fought the panic rising in her throat.

Kathy squeezed her shoulder. "I'm worried about you, honey. You're too young to have to do all this on your own."

Elisabeth filled three glasses with ice and placed them on the tray. She had managed against bad odds before and would do it again now. Tears stung her eyes, and she blinked them away. "I don't have a choice."

"You need a break." Kathy picked up the tray. "I'll take their orders, and you deliver the food when you return."

"Excuse me," a female voice said.

Elisabeth turned and saw the stylishly dressed blond from table four. The engagement ring on her finger could have paid off the second mortgage on the farm and put at least two of her siblings through college. "I was wondering if you could bring some extra napkins with the bottled water?"

"I'll take care of it, miss." Kathy glanced at Elisabeth. "Get some fresh air."

She knew better than to argue with her boss, especially in front of a customer. Elisabeth needed a few minutes alone. She stepped outside, took a deep breath, and let the tears flow.

When Elisabeth returned to the kitchen, she was surprised to see Kathy and the customer from table four talking. The tray still sat on the counter, though napkins had been added next to the plate of lemons, a bottle of water, and three glasses. As soon as they noticed her, they stopped chatting.

"Feel better after your break?" Kathy asked.

Elisabeth didn't often allow herself the luxury of tears, because she was afraid once she started crying, she wouldn't be able to stop. And this job was too important to let a pity party ruin her tips for the rest of her shift. "Yes."

"You'll feel even better in a few minutes." Kathy picked up the tray. "Elisabeth Wheeler, this is Cynthia Sterling. I do believe she's the answer to your prayers."

With that, Kathy left the kitchen.

Elisabeth wasn't sure what was happening, but the beautiful blond woman wearing designer clothes wasn't a guardian angel. And she'd stopped believing in fairy godmothers a long time ago.

Cynthia stepped toward her, and Elisabeth noticed the woman favoring her left foot. "When I walked past the kitchen, I overheard you needed someone to help with your farm."

Elisabeth nodded. "Someone" about covered what she was looking for. If the person wasn't dangerous and a menace to society, she would hire them.

"I apologize for eavesdropping, but Kathy told me a little more about your situation after you left. I'm sorry."

Elisabeth hated pity. She'd faced it from friends, neighbors, and even strangers for too long.

"I want to help," Cynthia said.

She wouldn't accept charity, and that was the only way the beautiful blond could help her. Elisabeth wiped the counter. "Thanks, but I don't see how you—"

"My friend Henry, sitting across from my fiancé and me, needs a job. He's a good man but made some bad investments and lost everything. He needs to turn his life around. Working on your farm would give him that chance."

She had to be kidding. The closest he'd ever come to country was wearing Ralph Lauren Polo Country. Cynthia's friend was dressed as if worth a million dollars with his leather jacket, lightly starched, perfectly pressed button-down shirt, and knife-edge creased pants. His hands looked as if he worked in an office not outside. "It's hard work. Manual work. Long hours outdoors."

"That's exactly what Henry loves to do. He's a get-your-hands-dirty type of guy."

Not the well-dressed guy at table four. No way.

Elisabeth appreciated Cynthia for trying to help, but Henry wasn't what she needed. "No. I'm paying my foreman while he's away. I can't afford to pay another worker."

"I'll cover his expenses and his salary, say minimum wage?"

Elisabeth managed to keep her jaw from dropping open. Henry would work on her farm, and it wouldn't cost her a penny? It sounded too good to be true. Things like this didn't happen to her. To anyone. "That's generous of you, but why don't you give him the money yourself?"

"Henry is a proud man who won't accept charity from his friends."

"I respect that." And understood it, too. She'd felt the same way since her parents' deaths.

"This would be the perfect way for my fiancé and me to help Henry. And you would get the help you need."

True. Still, this whole situation felt…off. How could she back out gracefully? "But—"

"Henry doesn't have a place to live," Cynthia interrupted.

Elisabeth had never seen such a well-dressed, well-groomed homeless person in her entire life. Of course, her entire life had been spent in Oregon and most of it in Berry Patch.

"He'll need a place to stay," Cynthia continued.

Opening her home to a stranger didn't appeal to Elisabeth. Neither did the assumption that Henry would be hired. No, this would not work out, regardless of how much work awaited Elisabeth at home. "I'm sorry, but I don't have an extra bedroom. I'm sure you'll find him another job—"

"What about a barn?" Cynthia asked.

"I wouldn't ask anyone to sleep in a dirty, old barn."

The elegant woman frowned. "I suppose not. Oh well. This would have been so good for Henry. He's such a fine man trying to find his way back." Cynthia's eyes glistened with tears. "I so wanted to help him."

Maybe Cynthia only wanted to do a good deed.

Maybe Henry was a good man. Maybe someone else would walk into the café and offer to work for free.

Elisabeth had doubts. Too many doubts. Something was definitely off with this whole situation. She shouldn't hire Henry. Cynthia Sterling wasn't a beautiful fairy godmother who made wishes come true like in *Cinderella*. No, she was nothing more than a well-dressed woman. A customer, a stranger. "I'm sorry, but I know nothing about you or Henry. I have my brother and two sisters to think about."

"I'll give you references to call."

If Manny were here, he would do the hiring. If Manny were here, Elisabeth wouldn't be in this bind. "I'll contact them, but I can't guarantee I'll hire Henry."

"What if I pay you?" Cynthia asked. "Say twenty-five thousand."

Elisabeth gulped. "Dollars?"

"No, lira." Cynthia held out her cell phone and showed an app to send money. "Of course, it's dollars. I'll refund your expenses and Henry's salary later."

For that much money, Elisabeth would sleep in the barn and give Henry her bedroom.

Stay calm. Think this through.

She had to have help winterizing her farm. She couldn't take time off from her serving job to do it herself. She couldn't afford to lose any of the equipment or crops. Not if she wanted to hold on to the farm. And twenty-five thousand dollars was a huge amount of money. That would make such a difference in their lives. It would change everything.

Besides, this guy wouldn't stick around. Nobody stuck around here for long, but that guy looked as if he'd be gone quicker than most. "What if Henry quits?"

"If Henry quits, you keep the money. Deal?"

Instinct told Elisabeth to take the deal and take a chance on Henry. But Elisabeth didn't like taking chances on anyone. She didn't like opening herself and her family up to more disappointment. They'd all been hurt enough. Henry could cause trouble on all sorts of levels. She already knew he was a flirt.

But there was the money to consider. And the kids. And the farm. "I need the references."

Cynthia typed in the amount, and Elisabeth stared at all the zeros. Twenty-five thousand dollars. *With that money…* Her pulse quickened.

"I'll leave the payment on the app. I can see you have doubts, so here's a list of references. Use my phone so they recognize the caller ID and answer." Cynthia gave her the cell phone with a notepad opened with names and numbers. "Tell them Cynthia Sterling is setting Henry up for a little adventure of his own and ask whatever questions you might have."

"Don't I need Henry's last name?"

"It's Davenport, but his first name will suffice. You'll find out enough about Henry to make up your mind." She held on to her small purse. "If you don't want to hire Henry, simply return my phone by the time we finish with lunch. If you will hire him, type in your payment account, your address, and the time you get off work onto the notepad so I can send you the money and we can drop him off."

"We could change our sleeping arrangements so Henry would have his own room." Elisabeth didn't know what prompted her to say the words. Sympathy? More like desperation.

"That would be perfect." Cynthia grinned. "Though I still say the barn would be fine."

As Elisabeth watched her limp back to the dining room, she clutched the cell phone and prayed everything went well with the calls, and that his references were solid. She hadn't had time for daydreams or fantasies in years, but today, she wanted to believe in guardian angels or fairy godmothers or winning the lottery. Anything to justify wanting to hire Henry if his references checked out.

And a part of Elisabeth thought they just might. Cynthia Sterling seemed like she could have a magic wand hidden somewhere on her.

Chapter Three

The food was better than Henry expected. And the service... Elisabeth with an *S* proved herself to be the world's best server. Whatever they wanted as soon as they wanted it. Nothing but polite words flowed from her smiling lips.

And it was torture for him.

Henry didn't want to see her nor hear her sweet voice. He wanted her to drop a plate, spill a drink, and sneer at him. But she didn't. And he found it difficult—if not impossible—to keep from studying her every movement. He caught another glimpse of Elisabeth's support-hose-covered legs. Not being able to keep his eyes off her aggravated him.

Definitely time to get her out of sight and out of mind. "Let's get the check. Frank's waiting."

Frank, his longtime chauffeur and bodyguard, would

drive them along the route Henry had mapped out for their day. Wineries for tours and tastings, and dinner at a new restaurant in Dundee. In a few short hours, the Berry Bistro would be nothing more than a memory.

When he was back home in Portland, he would make seven different dates for next week—one for each night. Nothing romantic since that wasn't what he wanted, but dating was like a hobby to him and would keep his mind occupied. That would be enough to slam the door on the small-town server and make him forget she existed.

Elisabeth brought the check and returned Cynthia's cell phone, who said she must have left it in the kitchen when she asked for more napkins. Cynthia grabbed the check, which was out of character for her, but Henry wasn't about to complain. She'd been so sweet to him during the entire lunch. It must be Cade's influence. A satisfied feeling settled over Henry. Once again, he was pleased his matchmaking skills were so attuned.

After Cynthia paid the bill, he stood at the bistro's entrance. The temptation to glance over his shoulder one last time was strong, but he was stronger. He walked out and slid into his limo. Cade followed him, but Cynthia spoke to Frank for a few minutes first, then she got in. The doors shut, and Henry breathed a small sigh.

The car moved forward, and relief washed over him. Someday, he'd have a good laugh over his odd attraction to a server named Elisabeth in a tiny town called Berry Patch. But not today. An award-winning bottle of pinot noir had his name on it, and he couldn't wait for a sip.

Twenty minutes later, the limo stopped, not at a winery but in a Walmart parking lot.

"What's going on?" Henry asked.

"I'll be right back," Cynthia chirped. Several minutes later, she returned with two large shopping bags, then they were back on the road. Using Cade's Swiss Army knife, she cut the tags off an assortment of clothing items, placed her purchases in a large navy duffel bag, and pushed it toward Henry's feet. "This is yours."

Henry furrowed his brow. "I'm confused."

"So am I," Cade said. "But these past few months, I've learned to sit back and relax, and everything will work out fine."

"You've come so far." Cynthia kissed Cade's cheek. "And now it's Henry's turn. It's time to experience your own adventure. You'll see it's not all fun and games. And that you have to stop trying to control other people's lives."

Henry laughed. "Can I help it if I know what's best for my friends?"

Cynthia tilted her chin. "By that logic, I'm your friend, so I must know what's best for you. Unless you're wrong about people knowing what their friends need most."

She and Cade were living proof Henry knew what he was doing. Laurel and Brett Matthews, too. Not to mention the Billionaires of Silicon Forest. It hurt Henry that Cynthia couldn't see that. "I'm not wrong."

"Then prove it. Go on this adventure," Cynthia challenged. "It's time to put your money where your mouth is."

Anticipation hung in the air. He glanced at Cade, who merely shrugged.

Henry couldn't expect his friends to participate in his adventures if he wasn't willing to do the same. But this was Cynthia. She didn't know what he wanted or needed. She also knew nothing about planning an adventure. Challenging adventures took time and careful preparation. He spent months working on his. Hers smacked of last-minute haste. He could handle whatever she threw at him.

"Fine," Henry said finally. "I'll go on your little adventure and prove I'm right. That I know what's best for my friends. And when I win, I get to plan your honeymoon."

Cade leaned forward. "Wait a minute."

"Don't worry, honey. We haven't gotten to the rewards yet," Cynthia assured him with confidence. "Your cell phone and wallet, please."

Henry handed them over. She removed his credit cards, his calling card, and his cash before returning the wallet.

"It isn't safe to carry all these hundreds around." She gave him one twenty-dollar bill. "Here's the deal. You're still Henry Davenport, but the only money you have left in the world is this twenty. You're broke, out of work, and homeless. You've been living off the generosity of your friends since making a string of bad investments."

Henry thought about his best friend, financial adviser extraordinaire Brett Matthews, and Blaise Mortenson, who also handled investments for him. "Don't tell Brett or Blaise."

Cynthia ignored him. "For the next month, you'll work and live on a farm. You can only spend the money you earn."

"An entire month?" Henry asked.

"Or less if the foreman returns from Mexico. He may not want to keep you on."

Henry's knowledge of farms came from old reruns he'd watched with the house staff when he was a kid. It wouldn't be that bad. Milk a cow or two. Feed some animals. Fix a broken fence. People paid good money to stay in the country and at dude ranches. This wasn't an adventure. It was a vacation. "What's the catch?"

"No catch," Cynthia said. "But if you spend any money that you didn't earn or tell anyone the truth about yourself or return home before your time is up or get fired, you lose."

Sounded simple enough. "If I win?"

"If you last the entire month, I will never say another word about your adventures or matchmaking again."

"And?" Henry always rewarded his friends for participating in his adventures. Selecting the perfect prizes was half the fun.

"And the Smiling Moon Foundation's Island Camp will be named after you, as well as our firstborn son."

Henry had donated the island where Cynthia and Cade spent their adventure to Cade's nonprofit foundation, but having it named Davenport would immortalize Henry. And if Cade and Cynthia named their child Henry, they would have to ask him to be the godfather. He loved being Noelle and Brecken's godfather. Both were so sweet and stared at him with such adoration and love. He wanted more godchildren to spoil. Most of all, he wanted to prove he was right and

Cynthia was wrong. "And plan your honeymoon."

Cade frowned. "No."

"Yes," Cynthia said. "But if you lose the adventure, your birthday parties and legendary adventures come to an end, and so does any and all matchmaking."

Henry's heart fell to his feet. "I've already planned the next one."

"Then you'd better stay on the farm the entire time."

How hard could it be? If Cynthia could survive on a deserted island, he could survive on a farm. At least he'd have a roof over his head and indoor plumbing. "I'll do it."

Cynthia hit the intercom button. "To the farm, Frank."

Thirty minutes later, the limo passed a wooden sign that read *Wheeler Berry Farm* and turned left onto a gravel road. They passed a deserted fruit stand on one side of the road. The limo stopped in front of a metal building with large doors hanging open. The barn? Henry wasn't certain since barns were supposed to be red and constructed of wood and have animals living in them instead of rusted machinery and dirty farm equipment.

He stared at a two-story dilapidated farmhouse. He'd pictured a white picket fence, a swing on the porch, and an older couple standing in the front yard.

Not...this.

The house looked solid but neglected. The anemic cream paint was cracked and peeling, and the green—or was it gray?—door had seen better days. A blue plastic tarp covered half the roof and fluttered in the breeze. One shutter hung haphazardly as if held by a single nail. At least the place had a porch. Get rid of the flaking paint, add a swing, and…it would still be bad.

A rooster cried out *cock-a-doodle-doo*.

Henry startled. He thought they only did that at dawn.

"Having second thoughts?" Cynthia asked, sounding amused.

"No." He was up to his seventeenth or eighteenth thoughts. But it was too late to back down. He wasn't going to live here forever. Only a month. Thirty days. Maybe thirty-one, but who was counting?

He didn't see an outhouse, which must mean indoor plumbing. He hoped.

Henry swallowed. Hard.

Cynthia glanced at her watch. "We're a few minutes early. The farmer should be here shortly."

As if on cue, an ancient silver-and-black Suburban roared down the driveway, spewing a wake of gravel and dirt.

Henry grabbed the blue duffel bag and exited the limo. He glanced at Frank, who had lowered his window. "Tell Brett to handle things while I'm away. Let Blaise know too. Have Laurel and Iris take lots of pictures and videos of Noelle and Brecken. Oh, and Dash has bodyguards, but tell them I want you to drive Iris and Brecken if Dash is at work. That'll give you something to do while I'm away, and it's less for Dash to worry about. He's been hovering, which isn't good for any of them. In exactly one month, pick me up here."

"Anything else, sir?"

"No." Henry stood beside Cynthia and watched the old SUV sputter to a stop next to them. The door opened, and he saw a foot. A foot wearing an ugly white shoe. Next came a nude support-hose-covered calf. "It can't be her."

"It is."

He'd known there had to be a catch. But not even Cynthia would... *Oh yes, she would.*

Cynthia snickered. "And did I mention you'll be living with her, too?"

Elisabeth jumped down from the SUV. She still wore her uniform, but she'd removed her ponytail. Flowing blond hair surrounded her makeup-free face. She flipped her hair behind her shoulder, and he felt as if he'd been sucker punched.

"Thank goodness you're not interested in her, or it could be a really long month. We'll be going now." Cynthia waved to Elisabeth and gave Henry a peck on the cheek. "Have fun and be a good boy. You wouldn't want to be fired on your first day."

Before he knew it, the limo headed down the long driveway, toward the road and civilization. He watched the puff of dirt follow the limo until it disappeared. He stood alone. Cynthia's first mistake. Henry sent his friends off in pairs. Of course, that was necessary for his matchmaking.

Unless Cynthia wanted Elisabeth to be his pair—his match.

An interesting thought, but one he brushed off. He wasn't up for a lifetime commitment with anyone. That just proved Cynthia didn't know him. But a month with Elisabeth wouldn't be so bad.

Who was he kidding? It couldn't get any worse.

Another car door slamming, laughter, and footsteps filled the still country air. Henry glanced at the Suburban. A little girl with blond ringlets ran around the front of the SUV and latched on to Elisabeth's leg. Her megawatt grin lit up her small face.

Another girl, a few years older than the first, with gold wire-rimmed glasses and blond braids, joined them. A sullen-looking, thin boy, who appeared to be older than both girls and wore a black T-shirt with the faded words *Trust No One* on it, shuffled his way around the truck and stood with his hands shoved in the pockets of his faded jeans. The defiance on his face matched the expression on his black T-shirt.

The trio of blond-haired females shared a striking resemblance. The boy had Elisabeth's blue eyes…

And that was when it hit Henry.

It *was* worse. A lot worse.

Elisabeth didn't look old enough, but the proof was right in front of him. She had kids. His beautiful server was a mom. And just like brides, Henry didn't do moms.

Chapter Four

Elisabeth's insides were coiled like a ball of string wrapped too tightly. At any second, she would unravel and fall apart. She placed her arm around Caitlin's shoulder. Holding her youngest sister's small warm body allowed Elisabeth to regain her composure and gather an ounce of much-needed strength. Something told her she would need every bit she could muster when it came to Henry Davenport.

His references had checked out. She'd heard enough about Henry from Cynthia's list not to worry about him murdering them in their sleep, but he was a pretty boy like her ex-fiancé, Toby Cantrell, and pretty boys were never reliable. They always left when the going got tough.

Caitlin pointed at Henry. "Who's that?"

"Caitlin Wheeler, meet Henry Davenport." Elisabeth tried to keep the corners of her mouth up when all she wanted to do was frown. "Henry, this is my youngest sister, Caitlin."

As he made his way toward them, a dazzling grin broke over his handsome face. "Sister?"

Elisabeth nodded.

Caitlin waved at him. "Hello."

He bowed and was rewarded with a giggle. "It's a pleasure to meet you."

"When I'm five, I get to go to Disneyland." Caitlin tilted her head slightly. "Have you ever been to Disneyland?"

"I have," Henry said.

He bent over, bringing him closer to Caitlin's level and closer to Elisabeth. Okay, he wasn't like her ex-fiancé, who never acknowledged her siblings, let alone spoke to them. But Henry was still a charmer. His nearness disturbed her, making her feel warm and uncomfortable. She wanted to step back but wasn't about to leave Caitlin's side. Elisabeth bit the inside of her cheek.

"Disneyland is one of my favorite places in the world."

Caitlin moved closer to him, surprising since she was usually shy around strangers. For the first ten minutes, that was. "Do you know Minnie Mouse? I want to see Minnie and Cinderella and Ariel and Jasmine and Tiana and Aurora…"

"What about Snow White?" Henry asked.

Caitlin nodded. "And the seven drawers."

"Dwarfs," Elisabeth corrected.

"Dwarfs," Caitlin repeated. "Oh, and I want to see Belle. Anna and Elsa, too. I want to be five."

"How old are you?" Henry asked.

She raised her fingers. "Four. How old are you?"

"Caitlin," Elisabeth whispered. "It's not polite to ask someone their age."

"He asked me."

"I did." Henry's eyes sparkled with laughter. "I'm thirty-four."

Elisabeth did a double take. He looked younger. Not that thirty-four was old. She would be twenty-five in a few months. But she felt much older.

"Do you like ballerinas and princesses?" Caitlin asked.

"I do," Henry admitted. "Do you think you could help me with something?"

Wide-eyed, Caitlin nodded. Elisabeth placed her hands on her sister's thin shoulders.

"I have a goddaughter named Noelle." Henry's smile softened as he spoke the name. "Her birthday is coming up on Christmas Day, but I'm guessing she'll like ballerinas and princesses when she's your age. Could you show me the kind of toys and dress-up clothes she would like so I can be prepared?"

Caitlin grabbed his hand. "Let's go to my room."

"I don't think so." Elisabeth wasn't about to let a stranger be alone with her baby sister or her siblings. "Henry needs to get settled in Sam's room."

"Where's Sam going to sleep?" Caitlin asked.

"In your bed."

Caitlin frowned. "Where will I sleep?"

"With me."

"I'll go move my babies and animals." She skipped to the porch, bounced up the stairs, and jumped inside the house.

"Cute girl," Henry said.

With blond ringlets and big sparkling blue eyes, Caitlin

was the definition of cute and knew it, too. Elisabeth nodded. "But she'll talk your ear off. She talks from the time she wakes up until after she's supposed to be asleep. I was so worried when she turned two and only said a few words, but those words turned into sentences and conversations in a couple of months. She's quite the linguist now."

Elisabeth babbled worse than her stylist while she cut hair. She was just tired and hungry after today's shift at the café—make that bistro. That would explain why Elisabeth felt off-center and a little dizzy. She'd been up before the sun, and her day was far from over. It had nothing to do with Henry.

Sam, eleven and perpetually bored, stepped forward. "So, you want to work here?"

"I'm Henry Davenport." He extended his hand. "You're Elisabeth's…brother?"

"Sam Wheeler." He shook Henry's hand, but mistrust echoed in his voice.

Sam acted like a dog whose territory was invaded. Manny might run the farm, but ever since their parents' deaths almost four years ago, Sam had been the man of the house. He took the job seriously.

He straightened his narrow shoulders and puffed out what little chest he had. "You know anything about farming, Mr. Davenport?"

"Sam," Elisabeth cautioned. She needed to work on the children's manners. Not to mention a million other things. How did women make it as mothers? It was going on four years, and she still hadn't figured it out.

"It's okay." Henry met Sam's wary gaze. "First, call me

Henry. My father was Mr. Davenport. And second, I don't know much about farming."

Sam shot her a why-is-he-here look. Elisabeth felt the same way. Henry might not be qualified, but he looked strong and healthy. All his bones seemed to be intact, and he was breathing. And there was the twenty-five thousand dollars that came with him. The rest would…follow.

Henry smiled. "Don't worry, Sam, I'm a fast learner. I graduated from Harvard."

"Harvard?" Eight-year-old child prodigy, Abby, perked up. "Do you think you got your money's worth from your Harvard education? After all, if you amortized the cost difference between a state university and an Ivy League college and added in an—"

"That's enough for now, Abigail." Elisabeth tugged on Abby's braid and hoped their financial situation changed by the time her sister was ready for college. At this point, none of them would be able to attend without scholarships and financial aid. "You'll have plenty of time to discuss higher education options later." Elisabeth turned her attention to Henry. "Abby's what you might call gifted."

"She's a freakin' genius," Sam added.

Elisabeth sighed. "Why don't you two check on Caitlin?"

For once, they both did as they were told. *About time.*

Elisabeth rubbed her lower back. She stared at Henry's face, unable to find any fault with what she saw. He wasn't so much a pretty boy as a classically handsome man. Okay, he was totally gorgeous if she wanted to be honest with herself, which she didn't. Every instinct screamed to keep her distance.

A mischievous glint shone in Henry's eyes.

"You're good with children." The words tumbled out of her mouth. Had he realized she was staring? Probably. *He'll think you like him.*

Unfamiliar warmth flooded her cheeks. Great. Now she *was* blushing. This wouldn't do. So he was good-looking. She could handle it. Elisabeth squared her shoulders. "Do you have any children of your own?"

"No," he answered quickly. "I don't plan on having any. Kids are too much work."

"But there are lots of rewards."

"I know. Parenthood is wonderful for many people," he said. "But not me."

She didn't like that. Nor did she get it. He seemed a natural with Caitlin. "Why not?"

"I'm not father material," Henry admitted. "Too much responsibility. Someone always counts on you to be there or do something for them. I like to have too much fun."

He sounded like Toby, a large child living inside a man's body. *Kids only get in the way. We'll be living our lives for them, not ourselves.*

She hated to call the job off when she needed the money so badly, but not even for twenty-five thousand dollars would she subject the kids to someone who didn't like them. Elisabeth stiffened. "If you don't like kids, this may not be the job for you."

"I like kids, provided they aren't my own."

She reminded herself he wasn't here forever. Only until Manny returned.

She sighed with resignation. "Welcome to Wheeler Berry Farm. We haven't been formally introduced. I'm Elisabeth Wheeler."

"Henry Davenport, but you already knew that."

His perfectly straight teeth flashed in a brilliant smile, reminding Elisabeth that Sam's braces were coming up. "Cynthia told me your name so I could check your references."

His eyes widened. "You checked my…references?"

"Of course I did. I'm not in the habit of hiring people this way, but I know enough to check references," Elisabeth admitted. "Manny, my foreman, usually takes care of it. But his mother is ill, and he needs to be with her. That's why I needed help. The kids and I can't do it ourselves."

"How old are the kids?"

"Sam's eleven, Abigail's eight, and Caitlin's told you she's four. They're good kids most of the time. Okay, some of the time. They have their moments. Will you be able to handle that?"

"Yes."

He wet his lips, and she had to force her gaze away from them. Strange. She wasn't in the habit of staring at men's mouths.

"What about your parents?" he asked.

Sadness washed over her. No one had asked about them in so long. Everyone in Berry Patch knew what had happened, but no one wanted to bring it up. No one except the state caseworker who checked in on her siblings.

"They're gone." Elisabeth met his inquisitive gaze. She

didn't want to talk about them. "Your references gave glowing recommendations. One person, Brett Matthews, seemed surprised by your…situation." That was putting it mildly, but she didn't want to hurt Henry's feelings. "I hope I didn't cause any problems for you."

"You didn't. Brett is a financial adviser," Henry said. "He must have assumed I was following his advice."

That made sense. But Brett had recommended Henry for the job, saying he was loyal with a heart of gold and would be a helpful employee. He added Henry was good with children and babysat Brett's daughter and another friend's newborn son. That, in addition to the money from Cynthia Sterling, had sealed the deal in Elisabeth's mind.

Geese flew overhead. One more sign autumn had arrived, and it was time to prepare for winter. Good thing she'd found help.

"Tell me about your farm," Henry said.

"I'm the fifth generation of Wheelers to farm this land. We have over a hundred acres of the most fertile land in the Willamette Valley. Some of the original homestead was sold off during the Depression."

She had a love-hate relationship with the land, but pride filled her voice. She hadn't succeeded, but she hadn't failed, either. Growing up, this might not have been her dream, but it was her life now. One she wasn't about to let go. No matter how difficult things got, she would make sure the farm thrived for her sisters and brother. They would always have a home to return to when they got older.

"Thirty acres are row crops—beans and corn. The others

are berries—raspberries, marionberries, boysenberries, and evergreen blackberries. We have a small vegetable and herb garden and a handful of livestock. A horse, a cow, a few goats, and some chickens."

"As I told Sam, I've never worked on a farm before."

He sounded sincere and honest. Maybe this would work out. Elisabeth hoped so.

"Cynthia explained that to me, but I'll show you what to do. And I'll be here to answer any questions. That is, when I'm not working at the restaurant."

"Sounds like you keep busy."

"I do."

"What do you do for fun?"

Fun? That word hadn't been part of her vocabulary for years. Yet with Henry standing right next to her, wearing a devastating grin on his face, she could imagine having fun with him. A lot of fun. The thought made her wish he wasn't going to be living here for the next month. "I—"

The bang of the screen door interrupted her. Sam stood on the porch, scowling. "Caitlin's on the pot and needs you."

"Be right there." Relieved by the interruption, Elisabeth brushed a strand of hair off her face. "That's my cue to go inside."

Chapter Five

Standing on the porch with the duffel bag slung over his shoulder, Henry steeled himself for what lay on the other side of the torn screen door. He wasn't expecting the Ritz-Carlton, but he didn't relish the thought of living in a dive for the next month. On rare occasions, he'd stayed in four-star hotels, but he didn't like roughing it. He hoped for clean and comfortable. Perhaps it would have the rustic charm of a lodge, like some of the places in Hood Hamlet.

As Elisabeth opened the door, the hinges squeaked. Forest-green paint peeled away, revealing various layers of blue, yellow, and orange. "My great-grandfather built this house."

Henry respected being surrounded by so much history and family. His own grandfather had left him a legacy. Instead of a farm, though, Henry had received a multimillion-dollar trust fund that Brett had turned into billions, and Blaise added more billions on top of that. Henry was happy old Gramps had been a businessman and not a farmer. Without his money, Henry couldn't imagine what he would do every day. He'd never had a job. Well, until today.

"It was a wedding present for my great-grandmother," she added.

"How romantic."

The faraway look in Elisabeth's eyes intrigued him. "I suppose it was."

She motioned him inside. As he passed her, a floral scent, like wildflowers, wafted in the air. The fragrance was subtle, too light for a perfume, and he wondered if it was her soap or shampoo. She bumped into him as he contemplated whether she preferred bubble baths or showers. "I'm sorry."

"My fault," he said, turning. He couldn't help but notice when they collided that she was soft in all the right places. His temperature shot up. "I was blocking the doorway."

They stood mere inches away from each other. A second passed, then another. He should move out of her way.

Or step aside.

Or kiss her.

"Excuse me," she said finally and pushed past him.

So much for being suave and debonair. This awkwardness wasn't like him at all. Must be the country air interfering with his gift of charm and sophistication.

As he followed her into the living room, something sweet, not floral but fruity, lingered in the air, making his mouth water. The delicious fragrance appealed to both his nose and his stomach.

"I need to help Caitlin. I'll be right back." She hurried up the stairs before he could say anything.

Henry stood in the living room. His first thought was that a tornado had hit the place. But the house didn't look sturdy enough to withstand gale-force winds. That meant the mess was most likely man-made. Or rather kid-made.

He glanced around. How could three kids do so much damage?

Old stuffed animals that looked like thrift store rejects sat on the couch. Bent and ripped playing cards were scattered over the scratched hardwood floors. Coloring books and crayons covered the beat-up and ring-stained coffee table. Overturned chairs were haphazardly tented with blankets and pillows. A stack of very old magazines based on the cover photos littered a recliner.

The magazines moved. Henry jumped back.

A fat, long-haired gray cat crawled out from beneath the pile. The feline's hypnotic green eyes focused on Henry, then it turned, fluffy tail swishing in the air, and bounded up the stairs. Henry wished he could walk out the front door and back home.

Not for a month.

It wasn't that long. At least that was what he kept telling himself.

Henry had to give Cynthia credit. He hadn't expected her to pull off a real adventure.

Elisabeth returned sooner than he expected. "The house is always a mess. I try to get everybody to pick up after themselves, but there's only so much one person can do."

"It has that…lived-in look."

"Lived-in." She smiled. "You're just being polite, but I like it."

I like you.

"You'll see how lived-in things get with kids around," she continued.

Stop now. Alarm bells rang in Henry's head. He needed to slam brakes on his feelings for Elisabeth. He understood his physical attraction to her. Beautiful, gorgeous, sexy, she was all those things and more, but he didn't understand why the rest of the package—server with a farm and three siblings—wasn't putting a damper on said attraction.

Sure, they weren't her kids, but with her parents gone, they might as well be. He avoided dating women with children. He worried about an innocent bystander getting hurt once whatever relationship he was involved in came to an end. And they always came to an end. He couldn't help himself.

A good reason to keep his distance from his appealing boss. As much distance as possible, considering he was living in the same house and working on the farm with her. No matter his attraction, it couldn't go further and wouldn't. There would be no flirting whatsoever between him and Elisabeth with an *S*.

Regret inched its way down his spine.

"This is the living room," she said, looking away. "We have a new TV, but no satellite dish. Not that there's much time to sit around and watch television."

The set was on the small size compared to his at home—thirty-two inches if he was being generous.

"The kids were so excited when we won the TV at Peterson's Electronics and Hardware store last month."

They weren't the only ones. As Elisabeth smiled, a dimple appeared on her left cheek and made him rethink his no-moms rule, but only for a moment.

So much enthusiasm for a run-of-the-mill television set. He'd been excited by his theater room back home with its cinema-quality sound system and screen for a couple of days until the novelty wore off, as it did with all his other must-have toys. "How did you win it?"

"We guessed the number of nails in a five-gallon water bottle. Abby figured it out. She was off by four. No one else was close." Elisabeth lowered her voice. "She's good with numbers. And pretty much anything else."

"What about Sam?" Henry followed her through a doorway and into a large kitchen. The white cupboards brightened the room and made up for the faded, peeling floral wallpaper. On the floor sat bowls of different shapes. No doubt the gray cat wasn't the only pet.

"Sam's a big help with the girls and the farm," she said. "But I don't want him to grow up too fast. He should be a kid for as long as possible."

The kitchen was a mess, too, with bowls and glasses covering the faux-wood Formica countertops. Breakfast dishes? He could only hope. The one pleasant item he saw was a pie on the stove. Must be what he smelled earlier.

"Help yourself to whatever's in the cupboards or fridge. I keep the cookie jar filled, but with the kids, you never know how many will be left." She motioned to a large ceramic bowl filled with apples, oranges, and bananas. "You're welcome to join us for meals. It's never anything fancy, but food is food."

His personal chef and Iris would beg to differ, but Henry wasn't about to tell Elisabeth that. "Thank you."

Her gaze met his. "You might want to wait until you taste my cooking before you thank me."

"I'll take my chances."

A tinge of pink colored her cheeks. He didn't know many women who still blushed. He liked it.

"The kids are a little too quiet," she said. "We'd better head upstairs."

The staircase was wide with a wood banister and carved balustrades. Photographs covered the wall leading up to the second floor. A picture of Sam riding a tricycle. Abby sitting on the back of a pony. Caitlin in the center of a pumpkin patch. Henry did a double take. "You were a cheerleader?"

"In high school."

"Homecoming queen, too?"

"No, but I was the Berry Patch Harvest Princess."

"Sounds better than homecoming queen."

"It was." Elisabeth's smile reached her eyes. The effect— stunning. "I got to wear a crown for an entire week and ride on a float."

"That does beat homecoming queen. But what is the Berry Patch Harvest, and why do they need a princess?"

"Every year, Berry Patch hosts a big harvest festival. It's a glorified country fair with a carnival, dance, food, and competitions."

Henry had never been to a country fair. It sounded old-fashioned but fun. Maybe that would be a good theme for one of his birthday parties, though he didn't know what kind of adventure would go along with a fair. "Will you be running for the title again this year?"

"I'm too old for that."

He wasn't sure of her age. She looked to be in her mid-twenties but seemed older. Must be her circumstance. "I doubt that."

"The cutoff is twenty-one, and I'm almost twenty-five."

Henry was ten years older than her. "That's too bad because I bet you were the best Harvest Princess Berry Patch ever had."

The corners of her mouth curved. She started to speak but stopped. Henry thought he saw gratitude in her eyes.

"There are three bedrooms and"—she pushed open a door—"a bathroom up here."

"Bathroom?"

"There's only one in the house."

But it *was* in the house. No treks to the outhouse in the middle of the night. He pumped his fist at his side. Cynthia would be so disappointed.

"It's large, though, with both a shower and a bathtub."

"Abby and I fit in there," Caitlin whispered from a doorway. A small baby doll was tucked under her left arm.

Henry stared at the little girl.

"Why are you being so quiet?" Elisabeth asked.

"All of my babies are sleeping in my new bed. Your bed." Caitlin put her finger to her lips and made a shushing sound. "We don't want to wake them. Do you want to be the daddy?"

Henry's jaw tensed. "Uh, not right now."

"Later?"

"Where's Abby?" Elisabeth whispered, trying to let Henry off the hot seat.

"With Sam."

She took the little girl's right hand. "Help me show Henry to his room."

As they walked down the hallway, Elisabeth pointed out her room. It was on the same side of the hall as the bathroom. Henry wondered what her bedroom looked like and how much he could learn about her from the way it was decorated.

No. Thinking that way was a natural reflex, and he would have to stop. A month-long flirtation might be nice, but not with the children around. Besides, if he fell for Elisabeth, he would prove Cynthia knew what was best for him. She didn't. No one did.

No one knew what he needed, period.

Not that it mattered. It was just the way things were and had always been from the time he was a child. Henry shook aside the memories creeping into his mind.

He had to concentrate on the adventure and focus. He was here to be a farmer, not a boyfriend. Elisabeth might not be a teenager, but innocence shone in her eyes. This woman would expect a commitment, and that was something Henry wouldn't make to anyone.

Marriage was to be avoided at all costs. His father had said the same thing about love. That was one piece of advice Henry had listened to. There would never be another Mrs. Davenport. His mother had been the last in a long line of power-driven, wealth-seeking, social-climbing women who married for the money-rich, love-poor lifestyle of a Davenport.

"And this"—Elisabeth stopped in front of a door with an *Enter at Your Own Risk* sign on it—"will be your room."

The door opened. Abby sat at a desk, stacking comic books in the one clear space not covered with paper and clothing.

"Hello," she said, then returned to the task at hand.

"Samuel Joseph Wheeler," Elisabeth said, "I told you to clean your room."

"It's cleaner than it was," Sam mumbled.

Henry gulped. He couldn't imagine what the room had looked like before. The after picture was bad enough. It made the living room seem immaculate.

Stuff was everywhere. Piles, stacks, clutter, you name it. Forget about looking lived-in. Messy described Sam's room perfectly. Disaster area worked, too. But Henry doubted any element of Mother Nature could be responsible for this amount of chaos. It probably qualified for the Federal Disaster Relief Fund.

Elisabeth gathered pieces of paper from the floor. "I'll be back after dinner to straighten it up."

Straightening wouldn't cut it. A dump truck was required to clean this place. There wasn't a clear space from the door to the bed, and the only flat surfaces not covered with junk were the metal-frame bunk beds, but the top was a blow-up mattress that appeared to be half-deflated.

Elisabeth continued to clean. "You should be so ashamed by the condition of this room, Sam."

"It's not that bad." Sam climbed onto the top bunk. "Better than the pink girlie-girl room I have to stay in."

"I like pink," Caitlin said.

Pink would be better than this. Lace curtains and baby dolls would be better than this. Think on the bright side. No need to pick up after yourself. That was one thing like home since Henry had a staff to do everything for him.

"Oh yeah." Sam pointed at a four-foot-high vertical column with clothes hanging off the top and out the sides like a multicolored cascading fountain. "I cleaned out a drawer for you to use."

So that was a dresser and not an abstract artwork of textiles and wood. Imagine that.

"We don't have a guest room," Elisabeth said.

"There's always the barn," Sam added, earning a glare from his big sister.

"It's fine." No matter how Henry felt about his accommodations, he didn't want to hurt Elisabeth's feelings. It wasn't her fault he'd underestimated Cynthia Sterling. This was turning out to be more of an adventure than he ever thought possible. He noticed Elisabeth's forehead creasing with worry. She didn't seem to care the action could create wrinkles. "Really."

She smiled, and a warm feeling wrapped itself around Henry's heart. "Why don't you unpack while I fix dinner?"

A home-cooked meal. That would be a great way to end the first day of his adventure. And if dessert turned out to be the pie in the kitchen with a scoop of vanilla ice cream…oh man. He couldn't wait. Whether or not he liked it, Elisabeth with her pretty face had wormed her way under his skin. He hoped her cooking would do the same with his stomach and take his mind off the rest of her. "What's for dinner?"

"Macaroni and cheese with hamburger."

"My favorite," Caitlin cried.

He searched for a polite word to describe the horrific thought running through his brain. "What a combo."

His stomach agreed and launched an immediate protest. Henry had never eaten macaroni and cheese unless he counted fettuccine alfredo. Wasn't it orange, and didn't it come out of a box? He couldn't fathom how to eat that with a hamburger. Wouldn't a bun and macaroni be overkill on the grains?

"I'll be sure to make enough for seconds," Elisabeth said, heading toward the door.

"Great." Henry forced a smile. Maybe someone delivered pizza out in the sticks. He did have twenty dollars.

Chapter Six

Henry couldn't remember the last time he'd unpacked his own bag. Well, there was always a first time. He unzipped the bag to find Cynthia had stuffed items inside without using packing cubes or any logic to what went in first or last.

He attempted to fold a white T-shirt the way his housekeeper folded them at home. On the third try, he gave up and shoved it into the drawer as best as he could. Reaching for another T-shirt, he felt as if he were being watched. He turned and saw three pairs of blue eyes fixated on him. Sam's gaze was intense. Abby's inquisitive. Caitlin's playful.

Attention had always been a good thing. He loved being in the spotlight and the center of attention. Until now.

Henry was used to little kids Caitlin's age and younger. Babies like Brecken, not big kids. He'd never met a female he couldn't charm, so the two girls wouldn't be problems, but the boy, a brooding tween, would be another story. Maybe this would be good practice for when his godson got older, but he couldn't imagine Dash and Iris letting one of their kids act like Sam. Henry would get involved before he let that happen with Brecken.

He picked up the forest-green T-shirt and took a shot at being friendly anyway. "Do you guys go to the movies?"

Sam tossed a small ball against the wall. "Nope."

"What's going to the movies?" Caitlin asked.

"You pay for a ticket and watch it on a big screen in a theater and eat popcorn," Abby explained.

Caitlin grinned. "I like popcorn."

"So do I," Henry said. "But you don't go?"

"There aren't any theaters in Berry Patch," Abby answered.

Sam frowned. "There's nothing in Berry Patch."

Thump, thump, thump.

The sound of Sam's tennis ball against the hardwood floor reminded Henry of a metronome. The bouncing continued, as did the staring. He didn't attempt to fold the next shirt and tossed it into the drawer. The sooner he finished unpacking, the better. Next out of the duffel bag was a pair of white briefs.

"Wearing boxers is better for your sperm count," Abby said.

The thumping of Sam's ball stopped.

Henry glanced at the young girl. "Excuse me?"

She adjusted her gold wire-rimmed glasses. "Wearing

briefs can have an adverse effect on a man's sperm count, as does riding a bike. The temperature increases and—"

"Thanks for the warning. I'll keep that in mind next time I'm shopping." Even though his top button was undone, his collar felt two sizes too tight. No man wanted to discuss his sperm count, especially not with an eight-year-old. He grabbed the rest of the clothes from the duffel bag and dumped them into the drawer. "All done."

"At least he's not a neat freak," Sam muttered.

Another throw and the ball bounced across the floor to Henry's feet.

He grabbed it. "Anyone want to go downstairs?"

No one said anything, so he tossed the ball back to Sam and headed to the staircase. Halfway down, Henry realized he was being followed. He continued into the living room. The sofa was clean, so he sat. Abby settled on one side of him, and Caitlin plopped down on the other. Sam stood, glaring.

Elisabeth entered from the kitchen. "It's time to feed the animals."

Sam groaned. "Do we have to?"

"No chores, no dessert."

As she stepped aside, the kids stampeded into the kitchen. The slamming of a door told Henry they were gone. *Thank goodness.* A moment of peace and no one watching him except Elisabeth.

"I hope they didn't bother you too much," she said.

A police interrogation would have been easier. Henry wondered if he should mention Abby's comment about briefs and sperm count but thought better of it. He didn't want to worry Elisabeth. "I'll get used to it."

"I'm sure you will." She wiped her hands on her pants. She'd changed out of her uniform and into a pair of worn-in-all-the-right-places jeans and a white T-shirt. Simple, yet stylish.

"Would you like to see the crops?" she asked.

Over the years, women had asked him to see a variety of things, but crops had never been one of them. Until today, he'd never thought about what a crop would look like. Now he would be working in them. Or was that with them? "Seeing the crops would be great."

She led him through the kitchen. Mismatched pots and pans covered the stove, but the counter was now clean. He noticed a black-and-white cow cookie jar in the corner.

"We don't have much time before dinner," she said. "But you can see a little before it gets too dark."

He stepped out the back door. A grassy area surrounded the house, and a rusted swing set took up one side. It looked more like a death trap than play equipment, making him wonder if the kids had had tetanus shots. A garden lay to the right, and beyond that, row after row of crops. The knee-high bushes were tied together.

Berries, he assumed. They might be beans. It definitely wasn't corn. He knew what corn plants looked like.

"These are marionberries," Elisabeth explained. "We harvest half our berry acres each year. The others are cut down to the ground to strengthen the roots as they grow back. You'll be helping me train them."

"Train them?" Henry asked. "Do they do tricks?"

She stared at him without a hint of a smile on her face.

He didn't get it. He was being his adorable, charming self, but he wasn't impressing her one bit.

Elisabeth pulled back the leaves to show him the inside of the bush. "Cane berries are trained to grow on trellises."

"Like grapes," he said.

"Exactly."

See, he wasn't without farming knowledge. Wine and champagne he knew something about. "There's a…" He was about to tell her about the château and vineyard where he stayed in France last year. Instead, he pointed at the stack of white boxes amid the berry plants. "What's that?"

"Beehives. We usually don't have them this late in the year, but the beekeeper hasn't picked up the remaining ones. We rent hives each spring for the fields to help with pollination, so the blooms turn into berries. It's extra insurance for harvest time."

"You don't take any chances."

"We can't afford to."

As their gazes met, he felt a tug on his heart. It must be her eyes. He was a sucker for baby blues.

"I hope you realize what you've gotten yourself into, Henry. We must be prepared for winter. When the weather is good, we put in long hours. It's hard work."

"I can handle it." Henry could handle anything for a month. So what if he got a little dirty. He'd think of it as a poor man's mud bath. Nothing like the ones he'd taken in Calistoga, but he would survive. The manual work would be good for him. With no access to a gym, he needed some type of workout. And he liked being outside. Not a bad gig, after all.

Elisabeth raised a brow. He didn't blame her for having doubts. She knew nothing about him. He looked forward to surprising her with his innate abilities.

"Besides training the canes, you'll be moving the irrigation equipment. We also need to keep the grass short between the rows of berries, so you'll be mowing. We use a tractor to pull the mower. Will that be a problem?"

His mouth nearly gaped. "I get to drive a tractor?"

She nodded. "Do you like to drive?"

Henry pictured himself behind the wheel of a large shiny brand-spanking-new John Deere with a baseball cap on and grinned. He wouldn't have to worry about missing his Lamborghini and Porsche while he was here. Though he rarely drove since that was Frank's job. "I love to drive."

"Good. We have lots of vehicles to drive around here— trucks, tractors. We also use four-wheelers to get around. Saves a lot of time since there's so much land to cover." Elisabeth stopped at a dirt path dividing the marionberries from another type of berry. "We also use the dirt roads to get equipment in and out."

He couldn't imagine what the equipment might be, but he didn't care. Talk about getting lucky. He was getting paid to drive farm machinery and ATVs. Maybe he should have gotten a job before. This wasn't going to be work; this was going to be fun.

"You'll also be spraying. Timing is critical during

blooming time, but not so much now. We spray before the rain hits to keep the berries from molding."

"I can't wait."

And Henry couldn't. This was sounding better by the minute. Working heavy machinery was a dream come true. Now if he could just get a little chummier with Elisabeth.

Sam chased a screaming Caitlin out of the barn.

Strike that. No chumming allowed.

"We should head back inside," she said. "I need to finish cooking."

"Anything I can do to help?" He never did his own cooking, but the least he could do was offer. No one would ever accuse him of not having proper manners.

"Thanks, but I have it under control."

Just like everything else in her life. His respect for her increased a notch. He wouldn't want her job for anything. The responsibility and commitment. Talk about overwhelming. Just the thought made him shudder. He'd stick to planning birthday parties and adventures and matchmaking his friends. Things he knew how to do and did well.

He followed her into the kitchen. The aroma made his stomach take notice. "Smells good."

"Tastes even better."

Henry's eyes locked on her mouth, on her full lips. They were unpainted and more beautiful than those of a supermodel. And he'd kissed many a supermodel in his days. He couldn't help but wonder what kissing Elisabeth would feel like. He shouldn't want a taste, but he did.

* * *

Dinner was over. Not an ounce of Elisabeth's macaroni and cheese with hamburger meat and tomatoes remained. Henry had helped himself to three servings and kept saying how delicious it was. Funny, but the way he acted made her think he'd never tasted macaroni and cheese before. At least he enjoyed it, and that pleased her. More than it should.

As she dished up berry pie à la mode at the counter, tonight felt like a typical Saturday night. The air vibrated with giggles and singing. Arguments erupted from the table behind her. Things seemed so normal, until she glanced back and saw Henry.

Nothing was normal this evening. Nor would it be as long as Henry Davenport was there. She was as certain of that as rain falling in Oregon's wine country during the month of July.

She placed his dessert in front of him and passed out the other plates.

"We have a tradition that my daddy started," Abby explained. "On Saturdays, we take turns telling everyone our favorite thing that happened during the week."

"You do this every Saturday?" Henry asked.

Sam rolled his eyes. "Not only on Saturdays."

"Weekdays, we talk about how our day went," Abby clarified. "On Sundays, we say what we are thankful for."

Elisabeth glanced over at Henry. "You don't have to participate."

"I want to."

He smiled, one of the most dazzling, genuine smiles she'd

ever seen, making her lightheaded. She must be more tired than she realized. That was the only explanation for her reaction. She sat, vowing to get more sleep tonight. "Whose turn to start?"

"Mine." Caitlin placed her spoon on her plate. "My favorite thing was the tea party I had with my baby dolls and Sam. We ate cookies and drank iced tea. I like when we have real food. Sam does, too."

"Only if it's cookies." Sam's face was tomato red. Elisabeth was tempted to thank him for playing with Caitlin, but he looked too embarrassed as it was. No need to rub it in. She could talk with him later in private.

"You're lucky to have such a nice big brother, Caitlin." Henry scooped up another bite of pie and ice cream. "I don't have any brothers or sisters to play with."

Sam squirmed in his seat. "I just did it for the cookies, sheesh."

"You can come to my next tea party." Two lines appeared above Caitlin's button nose. "Sam, is it okay if he comes?"

Sam shrugged. "Whatever. As long as there are enough cookies for me."

He focused a little too hard on the dessert in front of him, trying to play it cool in front of Henry. Maybe having another male around would be good for Sam.

"I'm looking forward to it." Henry smiled at Sam. "Like you, I'm always up for cookies. Especially chocolate chip."

His sincere tone made Elisabeth believe he was being honest. Sam stopped shifting in his chair, so he must have believed Henry, too.

For a man who didn't think he was father material, he sure had a way with kids. And it wasn't only that. She'd never met anyone like Henry. Nothing seemed to faze him. Oh, that grin of his faltered when he saw Sam's room, but within seconds, it had returned. He seemed to enjoy whatever life threw at him. At least he had so far. Tomorrow, when he had to work, might be a different story.

"You're next, Sam," Abby said, then shoved a spoonful of ice cream into her mouth.

"My favorite thing was seeing Aaron's skateboarding accident. Blood was everywhere." Sam mimicked the crash. "It was so cool."

Boys. Elisabeth grimaced. Maybe if she were eleven… She didn't think so. "No one repeat this to Aaron, okay?"

Everyone nodded.

"It's my turn," Henry said. "My favorite thing was meeting a nice family who lives on a farm in Berry Patch."

"Do we know them?" Caitlin asked.

"He means us, dorkface," Sam muttered.

Elisabeth narrowed her eyes. "Language, Samuel."

He nodded.

"I'm happy to be here, and I can't wait to get to know all of you." Henry looked at each of the kids, then his gaze rested upon Elisabeth.

Especially you.

She thought he'd spoken the words out loud but realized his mouth hadn't said them, his eyes had. She wanted to look away but couldn't. She'd never felt anything like it, not even with Toby, and she wasn't sure if she wanted to feel it ever again. Uncertain, excited, nervous. Her emotions were as varied as the lunch menu at the bistro.

Heat spread through her. It burned, and she didn't like it. She took a bite of ice cream. Not that one spoonful would help. She would need the entire half gallon to cool herself down.

And once she cooled down, she could not allow this to happen again. She would have to be careful where Henry was concerned. Her life wasn't her own. She had no time for romance or fanciful thoughts. No time to chase her own dreams. Her responsibility was to the children and the farm. It was what her parents would have wanted and expected. So why was the truth suddenly so disappointing?

"I'm next." Abby's eyes danced with excitement. "My favorite thing was being the second person picked for Madison Patrick's team. I was the right fielder for most of the game, but I got to pitch at the end and struck Danielle McLean out."

"That's great." Elisabeth forgot about her own troubles and clapped her hands. "Now tell us everything that happened. Don't leave out any details."

As Abby described the game and events leading up to it, Elisabeth relished her sister's success. Abby's biggest wish was for her athletic ability to match her intellect. She wasn't the most coordinated kid, but she gave it her all. Some kids didn't care about that. To them, Abigail Wheeler was simply the class brain with glasses and the last one to be picked for a team— any team.

"Why didn't you tell us before?" Elisabeth asked.

"I wanted to save it for tonight." Abby grinned. "You're next."

"Let's see." Elisabeth was tempted to say finding Henry, but she didn't want to give him the wrong impression. Not that he thought that way about her. Still, she couldn't forget how he had stared at her a few minutes ago. Her pulse raced thinking about it. That was warning enough. Henry should not be her favorite thing. She had to remember what was most important—her brother and sisters. Toby had said no man would want all the extra baggage she brought into a relationship. And so far, he'd been proven right. But Elisabeth didn't care. She wanted her siblings and loved them more than anything. And would continue to do so.

Henry might say he loved children so long as they weren't his while being charming to them, but the charm would fade. And he would leave. At least the kids hadn't really liked Toby.

"My favorite thing happened tonight," she said, finally. "It was sitting here listening to all of you."

Sam groaned. "You always say that."

"It's the truth." And it was. More than anything, Elisabeth wanted to make this a happy home for her brother and sisters. Nothing gave her more pleasure than listening to their favorite things, even if it turned out to be seeing Aaron Eliot's blood.

"And sweet." The look in Henry's eyes was anything but sugary and sweet. "Just like you."

"And the pie," Caitlin added.

He laughed. The deep, rich sound rumbled its way straight to Elisabeth's heart. Forget about more ice cream. She needed a tall glass of water with lots of ice. He winked at her. Her blood started to boil. Make that a pitcher or, better yet, a water tower full.

Chapter Seven

Water wasn't Henry's normal nightcap, but it was better than juice. Or milk. With a glass in hand, he went into the living room.

Saturday night on the farm was quiet, peaceful, and boring. One night of this would be fine. But thirty? Forget it. Somehow, he would have to liven things up.

Not only for him but also for Elisabeth.

She'd been cleaning ever since the kids went to bed. First the dishes—by hand because they had no dishwasher—then the kitchen, and now the living room.

He wasn't sure how he could help her—his housekeeper cleaned for him—but Elisabeth paid him to work, not sit around. "Do you want some help?"

"I'm almost done, but thanks." She folded a pastel rainbow-colored afghan and laid it over the back of the couch.

"You should relax. Get used to being here. After tonight, you'll have a lot of work to do."

He didn't consider driving a tractor work, but he appreciated the hospitality. She had gone out of her way to make him feel welcome, even though he was bunking in an eleven-year-old's personal landfill.

Henry sat on the old recliner. It was comfortable despite the rips and tears and scribbles with colored markers on the tan-colored upholstery. He took a sip of water and set his glass on the maple end table next to the milk-jug lamp Caitlin had shown him how to turn on with a clap of his hands. This place was going to take some getting used to.

Henry leaned back and studied the photos on the fireplace mantel. One picture caught his eye. A baby wrapped in a blue blanket was being held by a couple. Sam, Henry guessed. And his parents.

It was none of his business, but Henry wanted to know more about the Wheelers. Especially Elisabeth. Something about her intrigued him, something beyond the way she looked, and he wanted to figure out what. "You said your parents were gone. Where did they go?"

She picked up a baby doll from the floor. "Heaven."

He should have guessed. No one would leave these children on their own with a farm. Henry struggled for the correct words to say. He had a reputation for being smooth, but smooth wasn't happening. He'd try sincere. "I'm sorry."

"Thanks." She placed the doll in a plastic laundry basket containing toys. He thought back to the playroom he'd had built for Noelle when she visited. She wasn't even two yet but had more toys than all three Wheeler children.

"What happened to your parents?" Henry was prying, but he didn't care.

Elisabeth brushed broken pieces of crayons off the coffee table and into a shoebox. "My father and stepmother were killed in a car accident on Highway 18."

"My parents were killed, too," he admitted, remembering the pain, the frustration, and the confusion that had followed. "In a plane crash."

She glanced up at him with compassion in her eyes. "Death is always difficult. My mom died of cancer when I was little, so my stepmother raised me, but it just seems harder when it's…sudden. Unexpected."

Even though he hadn't been close to his parents, it had been a difficult time for Henry. If not for Brett and Laurel and Cynthia and his other friends… Henry owed them so much. Sending them on adventures had been an easy way to pay them back. And he was an excellent matchmaker. "You must have been so young when this happened."

"I turned twenty-one two weeks before the accident."

Words failed Henry at the responsibility facing her. Then and now. His life paled in comparison. So did he. He avoided responsibility as much as possible, while she grabbed it with both hands. "You were so young. You're still so young."

"I feel much older than twenty-four. The kids are growing up so fast." Elisabeth kneeled and picked up multicolored LEGO bricks from the braided rug covering the hardwood floor. "One of these days, I'm going to look up, and they'll be heading off to college."

"Did you go to college?"

"Yes, but I didn't finish." She sounded so nonchalant, but the longing in her eyes told Henry she was far from indifferent. He couldn't imagine giving up everything for someone else, even if they were relatives.

"Why don't you go back?" he asked.

"The kids, the farm, my job. Maybe once Caitlin starts school, I'll think about it." Elisabeth should be complaining, but she wasn't.

"Do."

"You're sweet to think of me."

She was the only one he wanted to think of. That realization should worry him more than it did. But whatever he was feeling wouldn't last. It never did.

"What about you?" she asked. "You've lost your parents and…everything else. Do you have plans for the future?"

Concern filled her voice, and Henry felt like a jerk. His plans involved birthday parties and adventures. A trip to New York for Thanksgiving, a vacation in Maui and Lanai for two weeks in January, and skiing in Telluride in February. "A few."

She didn't appear convinced. "Once Manny gets back, I won't need your help."

"I know."

"I have a computer. It's old, but you could put together a résumé."

"Thanks."

Henry was ten years older than she was, but he'd never had to face what she faced daily. He tried to imagine what her life had been like. One minute, a college student, the next, a parent for three orphans and an orphan herself. Quitting school to take care of her siblings. Running a farm. Working at a restaurant. "Why do you waitress if you have the farm?"

"Farming isn't the easiest way to make a living. You never know how the crops will do or how much they will be worth. That's why we plant row crops in addition to the cane berries. Don't want to have all my eggs in one basket." She reached under the table for a red LEGO piece. "And Kathy provides benefits."

"Benefits?"

"Medical and dental insurance," Elisabeth explained. "It's hard to find jobs with benefits in a town this size."

So practical, so sensible, so mature. At only twenty-four. Hard to believe. He had insurance but didn't know what it covered. Brett had set him up with everything, so he knew whatever policy he had was more than sufficient.

She put a lid on the plastic container holding the LEGO bricks. "Your job doesn't come with any benefits."

"I assumed since it paid minimum wage, benefits weren't part of the package."

"They aren't." She rose and placed the container in the toy basket. "If workers come back year after year, I try to pay them more, but it's never enough for their hard work. They deserve so much more than I can afford."

Elisabeth deserved more than working her life away in order to take care of her family and farm. This amazing young woman was so much more than he could have ever imagined when he first saw her this morning. Forget about putting her in a French maid outfit. Nothing less than a halo and wings would do.

"What about you?" he asked.

She picked up something brown and stuffed—a raggedy teddy bear with a missing ear and ink-drawn eyes. "Me?"

"What do you deserve?"

She clutched the bear to her chest. "I've gotten exactly what I deserve."

Henry didn't like the flatness of her tone or the way her eyes darkened. "That doesn't sound good."

"It's been a long day." She set the bear on top of the other toys in the basket. "There. A little less lived-in."

"A lot less lived-in." He appreciated her effort.

Elisabeth's grin lit up her face. He already thought she was gorgeous, but at that moment, she was breathtaking. He'd never seen anything more lovely in all his life. His heart skipped a beat. Three, actually. But who was counting?

"Ready for bed?" she asked.

The air whooshed from Henry's lungs. He didn't move. He couldn't move, couldn't think, couldn't breathe. It was a moment like no other, and he wanted to hang on to it for as long as possible. He wasn't sure what was happening. Something told him he didn't want to know. He'd been propositioned before, but this was totally unexpected. Yet welcome. Very, very welcome.

He raised a brow. "Isn't it a little early for…bed?"

"Morning will be here before you know it. And there's so much I want to do with you…"

Henry grinned in anticipation.

"Tomorrow."

Disappointment shot through him. Elisabeth wasn't propositioning him. She was talking about sleeping.

She glanced back from the staircase. "Are you coming?"

Was he?

Henry had to decide what he wanted here. Yes, he wanted to prove a point to Cynthia, but winning or losing his adventure wasn't the only thing at stake. Somebody could get hurt. Not him. Surely, he was impervious to big blue eyes and soft kissable lips and a slow sweet smile that...

Yeah, he was impervious to all that. But he could hurt her. Elisabeth.

Or—the idea seized him—he could help her.

Maybe he was meant to help her.

Elisabeth needed so much more than a date or boyfriend or even a husband. And it wasn't only her. Her brother and sisters were in need, too. The Wheeler family didn't need a farmhand; they needed a fairy godfather.

And Henry knew the perfect man for the job.

* * *

"He's gotta be dead."

No, Henry wasn't dead. But death didn't sound so bad to him. He'd only closed his eyes a few minutes ago, and now *they* wanted him to get out of bed. Not even fairy godfathers got up this early.

"If he isn't dead," the high voice he guessed belonged to Caitlin said, "why isn't he moving?"

Because I'm trying to sleep.

Henry didn't want to move; he didn't want to open his eyes. He wanted only for them to go away. Far, far away.

"No one can stay still that long."

Curiosity got the better of him. He pried open his heavy eyelids and was assaulted by bright white light.

He squinted, but that did no good. A jagged pain shot through his head, ricocheting off every nerve ending, brain cell, and whatever else was inside there. He squeezed his eyes shut. Not even his worst hangover had felt this bad. That was what he got for sleeping without a feather pillow. And these sheets were not Egyptian cotton. A poly-cotton blend, no doubt.

"You're finally awake." The soothing tone of a feminine voice seeped into his foggy brain and made him feel better. He'd fallen asleep, thinking about her voice. Her.

Elisabeth.

He forced his eyes open. Four pairs of much too clear, much too bright blue eyes stared at him. Henry glanced around for a clock but saw only a candy bar wrapper, a pile of comic books, and stacks of cards—baseball and monster creatures. "What time is it?"

"Seven," Elisabeth said.

In the morning? Henry couldn't remember the last time he'd woken up before nine o'clock. He slept late unless he had a plane to catch or an event to attend. And he always tried to schedule those at decent hours. He cleared his dry, scratchy throat and wished he could do the same with his tired, muddled brain. "Is this what time you normally get up?"

"Usually, it's earlier," Abby said.

Any earlier and they might as well not go to bed. Henry never fell asleep until after one o'clock in the morning. "Even on weekends?"

"On Saturdays, we sometimes sleep in until seven thirty

or eight," Elisabeth said. "It depends on what we need to get done."

Sam rolled his eyes. "She means chores."

Okay, Henry just realized a big downside to farming. He would have to adjust his hours.

"Would you like to go to church with us?" Elisabeth asked.

Henry thought for a moment. "Is someone getting married?"

"No," she said.

He sat up and hit his head on the upper bunk. Rubbing his throbbing forehead, he lay down. "Did someone die?"

"No," Abby said.

"Baptism?"

Another no, this time from Sam.

"Then why are you going to church?" he asked.

"It's Sunday," Caitlin answered.

Sunday meant sleeping even later than he normally did. It meant eating brunch and sipping mimosas. What he wouldn't give for a cappuccino right now. Forget that, he wanted more sleep.

"There's breakfast afterward," Abby said. "Mayor Logan makes her famous buttermilk pancakes."

Henry adjusted the covers. "Thanks, but I'll pass."

"No problem," Elisabeth said. "I'll leave a list of things for you to do while we're gone."

"Fine." Top of his to-do list was going back to sleep.

"See you later," she said.

"Later." He buried his head against the pillow, closed his eyes, and half waved. Much later.

Chapter Eight

Eleven o'clock, and Elisabeth was exhausted, more mentally than physically, but she still had a full day of chores ahead of her. That didn't bode well. She ushered the kids out of the Suburban. Word of her new hired hand had spread faster than mold growing on berries. As soon as she'd entered the church, the barrage of questions had made her want to turn and run home.

She didn't know enough about Henry Davenport to provide adequate answers, which only added to her friends' and neighbors' concerns. It was difficult when everyone in Berry Patch considered themselves extended family.

But she couldn't worry about them. Elisabeth had her hands full with her own family. They had to be her only concern. Not small-town curiosity. Not her gawking, lovesick behavior this morning in Sam's bedroom.

Heaven help her.

Seeing the shadows of Henry's lashes on his cheeks, the scruff of whiskers on his face, and the rise and fall of his bare chest had made Elisabeth feel all fluttery inside. But fluttery didn't cut it. Not one bit. That was why she concentrated extra hard on Pastor Haskell's sermon this morning.

Caitlin tugged on her hand. "Let's play in the creek!"

"What creek?" Elisabeth asked.

Caitlin pointed at a stream of water rushing from her vegetable garden. "That one."

"Oh no." Elisabeth ran, squishing through the mud and pooling water in her only pair of dress shoes. Forget about the shoes. They were dirty, but that was the least of her problems. She would have to replant because they lived off the food they grew, even during the rainy autumn and winter seasons. She shut off the spigot.

How could this have happened? Turning off the water was the first thing on her to-do list for Henry.

"Is it bad?" Sam asked, his voice quieter than usual.

Yes, it was bad, but the kids didn't need to know the truth. Life was hard enough for them already.

She struggled against the frustration seizing control of her. She couldn't lose it. Not in front of her brother and sisters. Elisabeth shrugged, hoping that put them at ease. "We'll have to replant a few things."

"I like to plant seeds." Caitlin bent over near the edge of the flooded garden.

Elisabeth reached for her sister. "Be careful—"

Plop. Caitlin fell knees-first and sank into the mud.

"Owwww." Crocodile tears streamed down her cheeks. "My knee. My pretty dress. And tights. Th-they're ruined."

Elisabeth picked her up. "We can wash the tights and the dress."

"I'm b-bleeding." Caitlin sniffled. "I need a bandage."

"Yes, you do." Bandages usually made any boo-boo feel better, whether they were needed or not. "When we get inside..."

"The house is on fire." Panic filled Abby's voice.

"Fire!" Sam screamed, only to be drowned out by the screeching smoke detector.

Smoke, thick and black, billowed out the kitchen window.

Elisabeth set Caitlin on her feet, away from the mud. "Grab the hose, Sam. Keep Caitlin away, Abby."

As Elisabeth ran to the house calling for Henry, her heart pounded. Everything they owned, including every photograph of their parents, was in the house. But so was a living, breathing person.

"Henry!" She yelled the name again. And again.

The back door flew open. Smoke, not as much as before, filtered out. The smoke detector fell silent.

Henry stood in the doorway, a burned towel in his hand. "Did you have a nice time at church?"

Who could think of church at a time like this? Elisabeth's heart rate had yet to slow down. Henry, however, seemed unaffected by any of this. That bothered her. A lot. Not to mention the fact that he was wearing her apron, and it was covered with...

She wasn't sure what it was. "What's going on?"

Her voice was steady and calm, not high-pitched. The house had been on fire, and she hadn't lost it. A definite improvement compared to her reaction to Sam's failing grade on last week's math test.

"I wanted eggs Benedict for breakfast," Henry said.

Caitlin frowned. "Sounds yucky."

Abby got a thoughtful expression on her face. "They say Benedict Arnold was a traitor, but there's compelling evidence to suggest—"

"Quiet," Elisabeth ordered. "What happened?"

"I was making myself breakfast," Henry explained. "I love eggs Benedict, but I don't know how to make a hollandaise sauce, so I figured an omelet and toast would be a good substitute. But I realized I don't know how to make an omelet either. Or toast. I'm not much of a cook. In fact, I've never cooked in my life."

His knock-your-socks-off smile sent her pulse climbing again.

Elisabeth didn't like that. Or him. He was so much like Toby, a boy who would never grow up. "First, you flood my garden, and then you try to burn down my house by cooking when you don't know how to cook. What's next? Do you have a swarm of locusts packed away in your bag that you'll let loose on the crops?"

He furrowed his brow. "What flood?"

"I asked you to turn off the water when you got up. It was the first thing on the list I left for you on the kitchen table."

"I was going to read the list after I ate breakfast." He stared at the singed towel. "I just got up."

Her jaw dropped. "It's after eleven."

"I generally sleep in on weekends."

Now, she was going to lose it. Her temper bubbled up. She bit the inside of her cheek and counted backward from ten. It didn't help.

Sam ran toward the kitchen door with a garden hose in his hands. Water dripped from the hand trigger. "Where's the fire?"

"I wouldn't call it a real fire," Henry said. "The flames only licked the ceiling."

"What's with the apron?" Sam asked.

"He was cooking breakfast," Caitlin answered.

"Doesn't Henry look like Daddy did when he wore Mommy's apron to make us cinnamon rolls?" Abby asked.

A rare smile lit up Sam's face. "Dad burned them."

Caitlin giggled. "Just like Henry."

Abby laughed. "The fire alarm went off. Smoke was everywhere. It smelled bad. Mommy was so mad."

Caitlin giggled again. "Just like Elisabeth."

The smiles disappeared. The laughter, too. Mommy and Daddy weren't ever coming home again, and it was Elisabeth's fault. A heaviness settled on her heart.

"I'd better put the hose away," Sam muttered.

Abby took Caitlin's hand and they followed their brother. "We'll go with you."

Elisabeth stared at the slumped shoulders of the three people she loved most in this world. No matter how hard she tried, she could never take the place of their parents.

"I'm sorry about the plants," Henry said.

Me, too.

Words weren't enough. They didn't have enough money to afford fresh fruit and vegetables at the grocery store. That was why they grew their own. "You'll have to replant the garden. We count on that food."

"Of course," he said.

As she turned, her gaze caught his. Looking into his eyes made her feel warm and tingly. What was she doing? What was she feeling? Henry was way more trouble than he was worth. She didn't need any more problems than the ones she already had.

"Is there anything you want me to do?" he asked.

"I left you a list."

"I'm going to get to it." He flashed a killer smile. "But I thought there might be something you wanted me to do first."

"There is." Elisabeth refused to be charmed. She squared her shoulders. "Clean up this mess."

* * *

Cleaning up his mess wasn't so easy to do. Especially when Henry had to use rags. Dirty, disgusting rags. He tried and failed to find a clean spot on the one he held.

"Do you have any paper towels?" he asked.

Elisabeth stopped putting sliced vegetables into a slow cooker—that was what she called it—and tossed him another rag. "These are more cost-effective."

That might be true, but they were also gross. He could buy a lot of paper towels with his twenty-dollar bill.

Maybe paper towels would bring a smile to Elisabeth's face.

She was upset with him. He might not know farming, but he knew women. The way she kept glancing over at him and pressing her full lips together were telltale signs. No problem. He'd gotten off to a rocky start, but he'd learned his lesson— no more cooking. Before the day was over, she would have a different opinion of him.

Henry scrubbed at the stovetop, but the burn marks wouldn't come off. At this rate, he would be there all day. Of course, that didn't surprise him. The only thing he knew how to clean was himself.

Until this morning, Henry hadn't realized how much he relied on his household staff. He was totally dependent upon them yet had taken them for granted his entire life. He didn't have to cook or clean or even pay his bills. Someone else did that for him. Someone else did everything for him. Whatever Henry wanted—from fresh towels to late-night snacks—was there when he wanted it. If he were at home, freshly ground coffee would be brewing, a three-course breakfast would be waiting for him at the dining room table, and Mrs. Zimmer would make his bed and tidy up his room. Even Frank kept the cars full of gas and running perfectly.

His life was so easy and carefree. Fun. Life on the farm seemed precarious and worrisome. A way to grow old before one's time. Not fun.

Elisabeth grabbed a bottle from underneath the sink. She squeezed the trigger twice. "Now wipe."

He did, and the marks disappeared. Henry couldn't

believe it. All that scrubbing for nothing. "This stuff is amazing."

"It's vinegar and water." She handed him the bottle. "You're not used to doing this, are you?"

He never had before. "No."

The expression in her eyes softened. "I'm so sorry, Henry. I forgot you don't have a home to clean right now."

"That's…okay." Henry felt anything but. He wasn't exactly lying to her. He didn't have a home to clean right now, and if he was there now, the last thing he'd ever do was clean it. He looked at the stove, at the sink, at everything except Elisabeth. "I've never been much of a housekeeper."

"I'll help you finish. We have a lot to do today."

Not only today. Henry had a month to make the Wheeler family's life better. That wouldn't be an easy task.

He stood on a step stool and wiped the spot where the flames had smudged the ceiling. The cleaner took the marks right off.

She handed him another rag. "Here you go."

"Thanks." His gaze met hers. She was lovely. If only she would smile more. But smiles and laughter seemed to be rare commodities around here. At least Caitlin seemed less affected than the others. He hoped the little girl remained that way. "Did I miss any spots?"

Elisabeth looked up at the ceiling. "To the left."

"I see it." After another spray of the vinegar-and-water combo, he wiped the spot away. "Got it."

She rinsed her hands in the sink. "Now we can really get to work."

Henry couldn't wait. Domestic chores weren't his strong suit. He followed her outside. "It might be better if my job assignments don't involve the kitchen."

Elisabeth's eyes twinkled. "I was thinking the same thing."

She showed him the irrigation equipment, and they moved it to a different part of the farm together. It was more physical work than anything and took longer than he thought it would. His hands sort of burned, but completing the task gave Henry a needed burst of confidence. He wasn't used to manual labor, but he was strong thanks to his personal trainer. If she needed muscle to help her out, he was her man.

Fairy godfather, he corrected himself.

Next up was mowing. Standing by the small tractor, Elisabeth explained what the various levers did and how the two brake pedals could be unlatched for use in the fields.

Sunlight glimmered off her hair as she bent over to double-check the hitch connecting the mower to the tractor. Once again, her beauty struck him.

But he wasn't here to admire her or be attracted to her. He was here to do a job. Two jobs. Farmhand and fairy godfather. Good thing the two could be done concurrently, or he'd really have his work cut out for him.

Elisabeth stood. "Any questions?"

A gentle breeze carried the scent of her toward him. He didn't recognize the subtle fragrance, but it suited her. Light, simple, a hint of flowers. Different from the expensive designer perfumes worn by the women he dated, but he liked it. A lot. "You smell good."

Henry realized he should have been paying attention to her instructions, not her scent.

"It's lotion." She looked away, but not before a charming pink tinged her cheeks. "The kids gave it to me."

Henry imagined a bottle of lotion and quickly pushed the thought from his mind. He needed to pay attention to what she wanted him to do. He wasn't here only to help the Wheelers; he was here to win Cynthia's adventure. Losing wasn't an option. No matter what it took, he would win and, at the same time, become an indispensable asset to Elisabeth's berry farm.

"The kids have good taste." Henry picked up the keys to the tractor. "I'm ready to mow."

The corners of her mouth lifted. "Think you can handle it?"

All he had to do was pull the mower between the rows of berries. A trained dog could manage that. Henry smiled. "Yes."

"Let me know if you need anything."

A kiss for good luck? No, he didn't need luck to accomplish this task. He wouldn't need anything except a cool beverage once he was finished. A bottle of Cristal would be nice. But he would have to wait an entire month for that. Even if he spent his twenty on champagne, he couldn't afford a bottle of his favorite bubbly.

Henry climbed onto the tractor and turned the key in the ignition. The engine roared. The machine vibrated and was way too loud. He loved it.

He hit the gas, but the machine didn't move. The mower

must be heavier than Henry thought. He gave the tractor more gas, and it moved forward. He tested the brakes. Instead of stopping, he turned in a circle. The brakes were unhitched. "Just checking the turning radius."

She nodded, but he saw the doubt in her eyes. "Be careful."

"I will."

She started to speak but stopped herself.

No problem. Henry would show Elisabeth how well he could handle this. The fun was just beginning. Not only for him but also for the entire Wheeler family. Their fairy godfather was on the job and ready to work miracles.

Chapter Nine

"It's a miracle you found Henry." Theresa Logan, Elisabeth's best friend since kindergarten, leaned against her brother Gabriel's pickup truck parked outside the barn while Abby and Caitlin played on the hay bales being unloaded. "Sounds like he's the answer to your prayers."

Elisabeth pushed a bale of hay to the edge of the tailgate. She thought about what Henry had done on his first day working at the farm and blew out a breath. "I wouldn't go that far."

"Neither would I." Gabe lifted the bale as if it were a bag of feed. Sam was right next to him, as usual. "I still don't understand why you hired this Henry guy. You had lots of people offer to help you when Manny left. Me, Dad, the entire town."

Elisabeth hopped off the truck bed. "People have their

own farms and businesses to take care of. I don't want to be a burden."

"You're not a burden." Gabe brushed hay from his navy-blue T-shirt. "Friends help each other. That's how it works. Unless one friend happens to be too stubborn for her own good."

Though she loved Gabe like a brother, she'd heard this speech before. Too many times. She wiggled the hay bale halfway off the tailgate, only to have Gabe take it. "Henry will only be here until Manny returns."

"You don't know when Manny will be back," Gabe said without missing a beat. "Henry is a total stranger. He could be anyone."

She climbed back into the truck bed. "I checked his references."

"The guy knows nothing about farming," Gabe countered.

He wasn't wrong, but thanks to Cynthia Sterling, it didn't cost Elisabeth anything to have Henry work there. Except her food stores, the paint on her kitchen ceiling, and her favorite pan. Oh, and their vegetable garden.

She pushed another hay bale toward the edge. "He's doing fine. Henry was a big help with the irrigation equipment."

"I heard he let the chickens out," Gabe said.

She ignored the niggling doubt that had been creeping up all afternoon. It added to the ones she'd had after arriving home from church. "I didn't warn him about the gate."

Gabe stuck his thumb through the belt loop of his jeans. "What about breaking the spray nozzle?"

"Henry offered to pay for the damage with his next paycheck." But as she said the words, she knew money couldn't buy back the time they'd lost after lunch. She was more behind than ever, but she hadn't even told Theresa what had gone wrong. That left the usual suspect. Elisabeth glanced at Sam. "What have you been telling Gabe?"

Sam jutted out his chin. "The truth."

All she needed was Gabe's doubts to add to her own. Still, she felt the need to defend Henry. He might not have known what he was doing—and he didn't—but he was trying. That had to count for something. Not everyone grew up on a farm. "It's Henry's first day on the job. Everyone needs time to adjust."

Gabe's gaze narrowed. "That sounds like an excuse."

It was, but she didn't dare admit it—not to Gabriel or anyone. Even if she feared Henry would never adjust. He didn't seem cut out for farming. He also didn't seem cut out for cooking, cleaning, or anything else. Trouble followed him indoors, outdoors, everywhere.

"Henry will figure things out." She said that for her benefit more than anyone else's. Twenty-five thousand dollars bought a lot of extra chances. Maybe she should ask Abby to run a cost-benefit analysis to see where the money and Henry's mistakes met. That point might be closer than Elisabeth realized.

Theresa glanced through a pair of binoculars the girls had found in the cab of Gabe's truck. "I know why you hired Henry."

"Why's that?" Gabe asked, visibly curious.

Theresa grinned. "He's gorgeous."

"I want to see!" Caitlin bounced up and down. Theresa handed her the binoculars.

Elisabeth forced herself not to sigh. "That's not why I hired him."

"Sure." Theresa winked. "I'm so happy to see a good-looking single man who isn't from here. The pickings are slim in Berry Patch."

"There are more than enough single women," Gabe joked.

Theresa rolled her eyes. "I'm sure Henry will give you serious competition for the most eligible bachelor title, big brother."

"I doubt that." Gabe glanced toward the field. "He's homeless and penniless."

"But with a face like that, I don't think any woman will mind." Theresa sighed.

Uh-oh. Warning bells clanged in Elisabeth's head. Theresa was a die-hard romantic who dreamed of finding her Prince Charming and one for Elisabeth, too. That's because Theresa fancied herself a modern-day version of Jane Austen's Emma. But what if Theresa wanted Henry for herself?

An unexpected heat surged through Elisabeth's vein. She wasn't the jealous type, but for some reason, a part of her wanted to get territorial over her temporary farmhand.

Caitlin giggled, staring through the binoculars at the berries. "Henry's so funny."

Elisabeth glanced over to the crops. Henry, sans tractor, ran with his arms flailing and swatting at the air as a dark cloud followed him.

Oh no. "Bees."

"At least he can run fast." Gabe shielded his eyes from the sun as if to get a better look.

"That's about all Henry can do." Sam snickered. "Except snore."

Gabe laughed.

"This isn't funny." Elisabeth hopped to the ground. "What if Henry's allergic to bees? We have to help him."

"Not much we can do except upset the bees more," Gabe said.

"He'll outrun them," Caitlin said confidently, still staring through the binoculars.

"What if he gets stung?" Abby asked. "We don't have an EpiPen."

"I have Benadryl in the truck," Gabe offered nonchalantly.

Henry slapped his arm and stumbled but managed to keep moving forward.

Gabriel grimaced. "I think he just got stung."

"Cool," Sam said.

It wasn't cool. Not at all. Elisabeth felt so useless, watching Henry try to outrun the bees. But Gabe was right. They could do nothing to help him.

"Even running from bees"—Theresa pinched her cheeks to give them color—"Henry looks attractive."

Gabe snorted. "He looks like an idiot."

"No, he doesn't," Elisabeth said, even though most other men did look like idiots compared to Gabriel Logan, who was ruggedly handsome with beautiful blue eyes and a grin that made women, except for Elisabeth and his five sisters, swoon.

"I agree. Not an idiot." Theresa combed her fingers through her short brown hair. "It's more of a run-for-your-life, I-think-I'm-going-to-die kind of cuteness."

Abby took a step forward. "The bees are slowing down."

"They must be tired of chasing him."

Henry continued running after the bees stopped. A part of Elisabeth wished he would run off her property and keep going.

"I can't believe he hasn't slowed down." Theresa sounded impressed. "He must be in really good shape."

Henry raced toward the barn. Sweat dampened his hair, beaded on his face, and drenched his shirt. Dirt covered the thighs of his jeans. His cheeks were red and his breathing ragged. He skidded to a stop, braced his hands on his knees, and leaned over to catch his breath.

"Are you okay?" Elisabeth asked, concerned.

He nodded. "Talk about a workout. They should add a swarm of bees to the Olympics. Bet we'd see a new world record."

She glanced at his face and arms but couldn't see any red marks. "Did you get stung?"

Henry stuck out his hand. Two spots were red and swollen. "They'll be okay."

She moved closer and took his injured hand in hers. He smelled of sweat, dirt, and fresh grass. The scent appealed to her more than it should. She released his hand. "What happened?"

"I cut a corner too close." Henry straightened. "The mower knocked over a stack of hives. I didn't see any bees flying around, so I thought I'd put them back."

"You never touch a hive," Abby said, reciting the rule the beekeeper had taught them.

"Never ever," Caitlin added.

He grinned. "I know that now."

Today had been nothing but one lesson after another for Henry. Talk about a learning curve. Elisabeth hoped he improved tomorrow. She handed him a spare bottle of water. "Is the tractor okay?"

He nodded and drank half the bottle. "The hives don't look damaged either, but I couldn't see all of them. They're still on the ground."

"Just leave them." Elisabeth didn't want him near the bees. Near anything. Maybe it was time for that cost-benefit analysis. "I'll call the beekeeper."

As Henry glanced around, his eyes widened, and the red on his cheeks deepened. "I didn't realize you had company." He managed a smile, and Elisabeth respected that after having made a fool of himself with the bees in front of everybody. "I'm Henry."

"Theresa Logan. Best friend and sometimes babysitter." She wet her lips. "This is my brother."

"Gabe Logan." His tone was wary, but he extended his arm.

Henry wiped his hand on his jeans and shook Gabe's hand.

Henry winced at the contact. No doubt the bee stings hurt. Still, he kept smiling. "Nice to meet you."

The two men were a stark contrast. Even with dirty and sweating and wearing jeans, Henry would be more comfortable in the city. Anywhere but on a berry farm. Gabe was outdoors and country-living personified whether in jeans or…

Elisabeth realized she had never seen him in anything dressy except on his ill-fated wedding day. After his divorce, Gabe swore never to wear a tuxedo again. But no matter what either wore or didn't wear, both men would be popular with the women of Berry Patch.

With women everywhere.

Theresa batted her eyes. "So, what brings you to Berry Patch? The bees?"

"The bees were a first and, I hope, a last." Henry stared at Theresa as if she were the only woman on the planet. "I'm here because a friend heard Elisabeth needed help, and I needed a job."

Yes, he was here to help her. Elisabeth's muscles tensed. Not flirt with her best friend.

"Sounds like fate." Theresa's voice sounded wistful.

Gabe frowned. "More like dumb luck."

"Probably a combination of both," Henry said. "Are you a farmer?"

"Contractor," Gabe said. "I have a remodeling business, but I help my father with his hops farm."

"Gabe fixed Old Yeller, too," Sam offered.

Lines creased Henry's forehead. "Are you also a vet?"

The kids giggled. Gabe and Theresa managed not to laugh.

Elisabeth frowned. Poor Henry. He wasn't having the best day. "Old Yeller is a pickup truck on its last legs."

"Rather, wheels," Theresa added with a flip of her hair.

Henry laughed. "Let me guess, the truck is old and yellow."

"Henry graduated from Harvard," Abby announced proudly.

Elisabeth cringed. Henry had to be humiliated. She caught a glimpse of sadness in his eyes, but the moment their gazes met, it disappeared. She gave him an encouraging smile, and Henry laughed. Laughed?

"Too bad my studies concentrated on romance languages and literature. Harvard doesn't teach you how to drive a tractor or outrun bees." Henry was so animated, his voice upbeat, his smile dazzling. "Wonder if I could get a refund."

Everyone laughed.

"I'm sure you could get whatever you wanted," Theresa said, almost breathlessly. Subtlety had never been one of her strong points.

"You think?" Henry asked Theresa.

Uncomfortable, Elisabeth ground the toe of her work boot into the dirt. Gabriel rocked back and raised a brow.

"Pretty smooth," he murmured to her.

Too smooth. Henry wasn't only a screwup. He was also a flirt. A charmer. A player. The job didn't matter to him. The farm didn't matter to him. She didn't matter to him.

He had to go.

But Elisabeth needed the money. And then she remembered.

If Henry quits, you can keep the money.

Chapter Ten

"Dog-doo, horse-doo, cat-doo. I've had it with doo-doo." Henry propped the shovel against the barn, stripped off his filthy gloves, and threw them on the ground. "Being a fairy godfather has never been this hard before."

Henry's new best friend stared up at him with sleepy brown eyes.

"You look how I feel." He rubbed the mangy mutt's head. Henry had noticed a lump of fur in a corner of the barn on his third day on the farm. He'd thought it was a dead animal, but the dog named Ruffian had only been sleeping. "Too bad there's no time to be tired. Only time to work."

Work.

Henry hated working. He hated everything about life on the farm. The never-ending exhaustion, the won't-wash-off dirt, the thin, sandpaper-like towels hanging in the bathroom.

It didn't help that he was the worst farmhand in the history of agriculture. So far, he'd done nothing but cause trouble and make mistakes. Mistakes in front of the family, their friends, and Elisabeth. She'd seen him get chased and stung by bees, pop a wheelie when he dropped the rototiller and nearly crushed Ruff, upset the chickens in the henhouse, break a day's worth of eggs, and fall face-first while mucking out the barn.

Henry turned on the faucet outside the barn and rinsed his hands.

This job was crushing his ego. Who was he kidding? He hadn't an ounce of pride left.

But Henry was all Elisabeth had. He couldn't let her down. Or Sam. Or Abby. Or Caitlin. Or Ruff. Or the nameless gray cat that now slept on his chest every night.

Quitting had never sounded so good to him. But it wasn't an option. Forget about faking an injury and spending a much-needed day in bed. He couldn't donate money and make it all better, or he'd lose the stupid adventure.

"It sucks, but I'm stuck." Henry dried his hands on a dingy monogrammed linen handkerchief that had once been white. "For a month."

Henry couldn't believe Cynthia had done this to him.

And one thing was clear. He didn't want to see how the other half lived. He didn't want to know how the other half struggled. He didn't want to be the other half.

If Cynthia was trying to teach him a lesson, he'd learned a big one. He was happy that he was rich and didn't have to deal with life like Elisabeth did. He was only supposed to be here for a month, but she faced this day in and day out. She'd done this for four years. Henry didn't know how she managed it or why she kept doing it.

He couldn't wait to get back to his real life. Once in Portland, he could do more for Elisabeth and her family as Henry the billionaire than he ever could as Henry the farmhand. "I could stay here forever and never be good enough for this job."

Ruff groaned.

"Don't worry, boy. I may not be cut out for farming, but she put her trust in me to do this job, so that's what I'll do." Henry removed his hands from the water. Dirt was still caked under his fingernails and embedded in the dry cracks of his hands, but that was as good as it would get. "Even if it kills me."

Which, Henry realized grimly, it just might.

Ruff's ears perked up. Footsteps crunched on the gravel, and Henry looked that way. Elisabeth walked toward him. She wore jeans and a red field jacket. Her hair was pulled back into a braid, and she wore no makeup once again. She looked more beautiful than any woman had a right to look. He only wished she didn't have those dark circles under her eyes that never seemed to fade, even after a full night's sleep.

Henry shoved the handkerchief into his back pocket.

She greeted him with a smile. "Good morning, Henry."

Seeing her made his morning better. Now if he could get his act together and do something right, things would be more tolerable. "Morning."

"How are you today?" she asked.

Bone-weary and hating life. His best effort wasn't good enough—for the farm or Elisabeth. Just like his parents had always said about him. This adventure was only proving the truth.

Henry forced a smile. "Just fine."

"You missed breakfast."

He'd fallen asleep after the alarm went off. It had been physically impossible for him to crawl out of bed, especially with Ruff dozing on his legs and the fat, nameless gray cat asleep on his chest. But when he finally woke, he skipped breakfast so he wouldn't start the morning behind schedule. "I wasn't hungry."

His stomach growled.

She removed something wrapped in a paper towel from her jacket pocket and handed it to him. "In case you get hungry."

Elisabeth was so sweet, always thinking of others. He unwrapped the paper towel and saw a rectangular piece of something. The white icing with red sparkles looked interesting. But edible? He was almost too hungry to care whether it was or not. "What is it?"

She drew her eyebrows together. "A Pop-Tart."

He'd heard of them before. They were Dash's favorite breakfast food, but Henry had never tasted one. He took a bite. Not bad. "It's good. Thanks."

Ruff nudged his leg as he ate, and Henry tossed him a bite.

"I can't believe the difference in that dog," Elisabeth admitted. "Ruff used to stay around the barn. He would only come inside the house to eat. Even during winter."

"He likes sleeping in the house now," Henry said.

"He likes sleeping with you."

Henry petted Ruff. "It's nice to have a warm body next to you."

"He's a smart dog." She smiled. "My dad found him when he was a puppy. Ruff followed him like a shadow. He loved my dad and tolerated the rest of us. Until you."

"Poor boy must have been lonely."

Elisabeth nodded and adjusted her gloves. "Are you ready to get to work?"

"I've been working since six o'clock."

"I meant working in the fields."

Just the mention of the word *fields* made his muscles tighten in protest. He would never look at a berry or any produce the same way.

"We're going to tie today," she said.

Henry didn't want to tie the canes. He wanted to kick the canes. There had to be an easier way. Like buying the farm from Elisabeth for an inflated price and burning it to the ground.

Stop. He couldn't think that way. The Wheelers needed help, and he was all they had. He had to get through this.

Henry put on a pair of new work gloves, hopped onto an ATV, and followed Elisabeth on her four-wheeler to the loganberries. *Try to look at the bright side.* He got to have fun riding from the barn and back. That was something good. Too bad everything in between sucked. He sighed.

Mist had settled between the rows of canes. Henry glanced up.

The sky was gray. Rain? He hoped not, but knowing his luck…

"It's not hard once you get the hang of it. I'll show you." With a paper tie in one hand, she reached around the berry bush with the other and secured the vine to the wire trellis without a wasted motion. "The canes grow so fast that if we get behind and they get too big, it takes two people to tie each cane."

"So we have to get it done before that happens."

"Exactly." She handed him a paper tie. "Your turn."

Henry took a tie, grabbed a cane, and threw the additional growth over the trellis wire. A cluster of thorny vines raked his face, scratching his left cheek. "Ouch."

"Are you okay?" Elisabeth asked.

It hurt badly. "I'm okay."

"You threw the vine the wrong way."

He did everything the wrong way. Everything except for his birthday parties and adventures. Without those in his life… No, this wasn't only about Cynthia's adventure anymore.

Elisabeth's eyes darkened. "Your cheek is bleeding."

"I'll survive."

Somehow, he would find a way to survive it all. The farm. The work. Her.

She took a closer look. "You should head to the house and clean that scratch."

"At lunchtime."

"Suit yourself."

He wished he could suit himself. In one of his Armani

suits to be exact. Better yet, a tuxedo. He had a dozen to choose from made by the top designers in the world. Anything to show Elisabeth the man he really was so she would see him as desirable instead of a fumbling idiot.

He was charming, sexy Henry. Women wanted him. Or at least pretended it wasn't his Davenport name and fortune they were after. But not Elisabeth with an *S*.

Even with his money, he wasn't the man Elisabeth needed. He was just all she had. He wouldn't let her down. He would prove to himself he was more than a fat wallet and a bloated trust fund. Henry focused on the next cane to be tied.

Elisabeth touched his shoulder. "Are you sure you're okay?"

Concern filled her voice, and his heart hitched. "I'll be fine. I just need to figure out the correct way to tie."

The corners of her mouth lifted. "I'll help you figure it out."

She stood behind him and placed her arms alongside his. Even with their jackets and clothing between them, he could feel the softness pressing against his back. Her sweet scent surrounded him. He wished they could work like this all day…

"Take the vine with this hand and toss it over the trellis like this." With her hand on his arm, she led him through the motion. "Now tie it onto the wire."

Henry had trouble breathing, let alone accomplishing any sort of task requiring brain cells. He wasn't sure how he managed to tie the vine, but he did.

As Elisabeth stepped back, emotion surged through Henry. An odd mixture of relief and regret. Holding her felt good, but so did helping her. If only he could do both…

"The bleeding stopped." Elisabeth removed her glove and touched his face. "I don't think it'll scar."

She stood so close to him and smelled so good it was worth a scar. Henry grinned. "A scar wouldn't be bad. Women find scars sexy."

"Some women do, but not all." She tilted her chin, put on her glove, and got to work.

"Which do you prefer? Scar or no scar?"

"It depends."

"On what?"

"The man."

It wasn't the answer he wanted. Henry wanted her to like him. Who was he kidding? He wanted her to want him.

What was he going to do?

* * *

What was she going to do? That evening, Elisabeth shoved a marionberry pie into the oven and slammed the door closed.

Henry should have been long gone. But he hadn't left. He hadn't slunk away in the middle of the night. He hadn't quit.

Elisabeth twisted the knob on the timer and overshot the time by fifteen minutes. She reset the dial to the correct time.

He was supposed to quit, not dive into whatever task she gave him. Okay, he wasn't diving. He was drowning. Still, he hadn't given up. Not even after she'd thrown in chores that hadn't been done in years like cleaning the barn, washing the equipment, and organizing the tools.

She brushed the flour off the countertop. Too bad she couldn't get rid of Henry as easily.

Why hadn't he quit?

That was the only way she could keep Cynthia Sterling's money and use it to hire someone who knew what they were doing. If any money was left over, she could fix the roof, the plumbing, and a million other things.

But that wasn't going to happen. Not now.

Elisabeth's shoulders slumped.

She had nothing left to use to discourage him or try to make him quit. And that left one course of action—to fire him. But thinking about firing him made her feel awful.

Elisabeth sagged against the counter. Not that she wasn't justified in letting Henry go. He had made mistake after mistake. She still couldn't believe he'd cut back the wrong row of berries, planted all the vegetable seeds wrong, and let the chickens escape again.

Farming clearly wasn't his thing. But even though he hadn't a clue about what he was doing, he was trying hard. That counted for something. She sighed. Twenty-five thousand dollars' worth of something?

She might be down on her luck, but so was Henry.

Maybe she could convince him to accept Cynthia's help—even take the money Elisabeth had received. No, he didn't want charity. That was why she couldn't ask him to quit. She didn't want him to know what his friends had done for him.

As she removed the lid from the pot on the stove, the scent of the Mexican stew with cinnamon, oregano, cumin, and jalapeño chilis filled the air. She stirred the simmering broth, added diced chicken, and replaced the lid.

The whine of a lone four-wheeler caught her attention.

She glanced at the clock. Henry had worked later than she expected.

Perhaps she misjudged him. Okay, he'd flirted with her best friend, but he hadn't destroyed the farm. At least not yet.

Maybe he wouldn't. Maybe he would learn. Maybe he could stay.

Her chest tightened. That reaction alone told her it was time for Henry to pack his bag and go. She couldn't afford to have feelings for a charmer like him. Not that she had feelings. But it could happen, and that would be a huge mistake. Henry might be here now, but she couldn't count on him to stay in the long run. Of that, she was certain.

The kitchen door opened, and Henry stepped inside with Ruff panting at his heels. He had removed his work boots outside and wore white socks on his feet. Dirt covered his jeans and jacket. A jacket sleeve had been ripped. His face had smudges, and his hair was damp on the ends. He smelled like he looked—as if he'd been working hard since dawn.

Attraction slammed into her. Elisabeth swallowed around the blackberry-sized lump in her throat.

"Did you see the sunset?" He stared at her. "Beautiful."

He was beautiful. Gorgeous. You name it. The simple richness of his voice made her pulse speed up. Another reason to fire him. "I—I didn't notice."

"I finished tying the rows you wanted."

"All of them?"

He nodded.

"That's good." Incredible. She thought it would take him longer. A lot longer.

And then it hit her. Henry had done a good job. He hadn't screwed up. He had been helpful today. Yet the last thing she felt was relief. Not when her insides reacted to his every word, glance, and movement.

Ruff nuzzled his nose against Henry. As he petted the dog, Henry grimaced.

Elisabeth took a step toward him and stopped. "Is something wrong with your hand?"

"A blister. It's nothing."

"You're not used to this kind of work. I'd better check it." She reached for his hand. A jolt of electricity shocked her at the contact, and she ignored it. He had two small blisters on his left hand and three larger ones on his right. "Why didn't you stop working? This has to hurt."

"The canes needed to be tied." His gaze met hers. "We can't afford to get behind. Isn't that what you said?"

She nodded.

"I know I've messed up, but I'm finally getting it. I won't screw up again." He paused. "At least not intentionally."

Yes, his hands were a mess, but that hadn't mattered to him. He'd put the farm first. And her.

She couldn't fire him.

Henry was staying. For now.

Frustration sped along her spine, followed by a surge of relief. It had to be about the check. There couldn't be another reason for the tangle of emotions she felt. There just couldn't be.

"Let's get your blisters fixed up."

Elisabeth gathered the supplies, then cleaned the blisters with antibacterial soap. "Does this hurt?"

"No."

She wondered if he would admit if it hurt. As she rinsed his hands with water, she noticed how large they were. He might not be used to manual labor, but his hands looked strong. And felt warm. She turned off the water. "Better?"

He nodded.

"You have nice hands."

"So do you."

What was she doing? Saying? They were just hands. Male hands. They were supposed to be big and strong and warm. She patted his hands dry, placed a dab of ointment on them, and covered them with bandages. Elisabeth put everything back in the first-aid kit. "That should help them heal faster."

He flexed his fingers. "Thanks."

"You need to be more careful." She focused on his blisters. "If you feel any burning or aching, stop what you're doing and see if a blister is forming. You also don't want these to get infected."

"I'll try to remember that." His gaze captured hers. "I don't always think things through like I should."

"That can get you into trouble."

"Sometimes it gets me what I want." He smiled. "Like now. I want to kiss you."

His words took her by surprise. She didn't say anything, but she parted her lips slightly.

Henry slowly lowered his lips toward hers as if giving her a chance to say no.

Step back, a voice in her head warned. Except Elisabeth had no room to do that.

One little kiss wouldn't hurt anything. Wouldn't hurt her.

Soft. His lips were soft against hers. And warm.

Henry didn't push. He didn't do anything except send tingles running all over her body. He cupped the back of her head and wove his fingers through her hair. She soaked up the feel and the taste of his lips. It had been so long since she'd been kissed.

Too long.

And she wanted more.

Elisabeth put her hands on his back and pulled him toward her. Henry took the hint and increased the pressure. Increased…everything.

He tasted. He teased. But most of all, he kissed.

Oh boy, she'd never been kissed like this before.

Her knees had never gone weak before. They were weak now. She'd heard of women swooning but never thought she'd be one of them. Thank goodness her back was against the counter, or she'd be on the floor. Maybe that wouldn't be such a bad thing.

Henry left no part of her mouth untouched. She didn't want to think about how he got to be such a great kisser. But he was so good. Maybe this was what they taught at Harvard. Maybe he had been born that way.

That had to be it. A natural talent for kissing.

She clung to Henry's wide shoulders. She didn't want to

let go. She didn't want this kiss to end. Not ever.

One little kiss wasn't so little.

Henry's kiss washed away her loneliness. She felt a sense of security that had been missing for way too long. She was no longer a big sister, a farmer, a server, a stand-in mom. She was simply Elisabeth. A woman. And she liked the feeling a lot.

He pulled her closer, and she went willingly. The years of wishing things could be different but knowing they couldn't faded. At this one moment, her life could be different. She could be different. She could believe in a happily-ever-after ending. She could believe in happiness again. She could believe in almost anything.

Henry backed away. His eyes were wide, his breathing as labored as her own. "I'm sorry, Elisabeth."

She was sorry, too. Sorry his kiss had to end. She touched her throbbing, swollen lips, wishing Henry's lips were against them, not her fingertip. She glanced up at him. "You're apologizing?"

"I shouldn't have kissed you."

No, he probably shouldn't have. But he had, and she liked it. A lot. He was ruining it by apologizing. "I didn't stop you."

"No, but that doesn't make it right."

But it felt right. So very right.

Henry glanced around the kitchen. "I work for you. I shouldn't take advantage—"

"Would you stop it?" She rose on her tiptoes and kissed him until she couldn't breathe. Until she couldn't take it anymore. Elisabeth tore her mouth away. "There."

He blinked. "Where?"

"You can stop apologizing. Now we're even."

But as she said the words, she knew that wasn't true. Henry might not be the player she imagined he was, but he sure could kiss. Suddenly, the farm wasn't her only concern. She had a much bigger one—her heart.

Chapter Eleven

Saturday morning, Henry stood on a street corner in downtown Berry Patch with the three Wheeler kids in tow, wishing he were anywhere but there. Portland, Prague, Paris. Paramus would be an improvement. But no, he was on a guided tour of a small town with an eleven-year-old who didn't want to be there either, an eight-year-old who knew too much about everything, and a four-year-old who had to go to the bathroom in every building they passed.

It served Henry right for kissing their sister.

All he'd wanted was a taste of Elisabeth, one kiss to kill his growing curiosity, not fuel his fantasies and make him want another and another.

Henry blew out a puff of air.

He waited for one of the two traffic signals in town to turn green and fought the urge to hit the crosswalk button again. Once he crossed Main Street, his tour would be over. He was tempted to run, not walk, across the street and straight out of town. That would be the only way to make the adage *out of sight, out of mind* come true. He had to get the constant thoughts of Elisabeth out of his head, or he would go crazy.

The light changed to green, and the *Walk* symbol illuminated. Caitlin slipped her small hand into his and glanced up at him. "I'm not supposed to cross the street without holding hands."

Abby grabbed his other hand. "Me either."

Sam sneered. "I'm too old to hold hands."

"You're never too old to hold hands," Henry said, wishing that was all he'd done with Elisabeth last night. He thought the farm work would kill him. He'd been wrong. Elisabeth was the one who would do him in.

Her and her kisses.

What was happening to him?

His reaction made zero sense. He'd kissed women before. More than he wanted to remember. But none had ever had a rock-his-world effect. He didn't like that she had, and he wanted it to stop.

"That covers downtown Berry Patch," Abby said with tour-guide hospitality after they crossed the street and stopped in front of the bistro. "Of course, the zip code covers approximately thirty miles of acreage surrounding the town, but it's mainly farms and vineyards."

"Where's Elisabeth?" Caitlin asked.

Abby glanced around. "I don't see her, so she must still be meeting with Mr. Jackson."

Sam scuffed his toe against the concrete. "She's never going to sell the farm to him."

The kids had been mumbling about that all morning, but Henry didn't know the backstory. "Then why is she meeting with him?"

Abby shrugged. "Elisabeth is too nice to say no when he calls."

Nice? Elisabeth wasn't nice. Did nice girls kiss as perfectly as she had?

"Maybe Elisabeth wants to marry him," Caitlin said.

The idea of Elisabeth marrying anyone left Henry feeling strangely unsettled, but then he saw a silver lining that might be a solution to his problem. If Elisabeth were kissing another man, she wouldn't be kissing him. If she weren't kissing him, Henry wouldn't be wondering when he'd get another kiss. He would be able to concentrate on farming and making life better for the Wheelers.

Sure he would. But anything was worth a try, and he was known for his matchmaking ability. "Do you think Elisabeth likes Mr. Jackson?"

"No one likes Mr. Jackson," Abby said.

"He's a mean old man," Sam explained.

Old was a relative term when it came to kids. "How old?"

"Fifty, sixty," Sam said. "You know, old."

Oh, that *was* too old for Elisabeth. An odd feeling of relief stole through Henry, given he'd been thinking about how he wanted her to be interested in someone else so she wouldn't distract him. Still, playing matchmaker wasn't such a bad idea. In fact, he tried mustering some enthusiasm. It was a good idea.

Look at his success with his friends. With the right man in the picture, Henry wouldn't feel so bad about leaving Elisabeth and her family once his month on the farm was up.

What kind of man would be good enough for her?

Someone the opposite of him.

The realization made him feel oddly hollow, but he knew what she needed.

Someone with lots of husband potential who loved kids. Someone who was handy and knew how to farm. And could love her the way she deserved to be loved.

"Can we do something while we wait?" Caitlin asked, sounding bored.

"Mrs. Showalter is having a yard sale." Abby adjusted her glasses. "It's only two blocks away."

Caitlin beamed. "I want to go."

"Like we need any more junk." Sam shoved his hands into the pockets of baggy pants. "Or have money to spend."

Henry remembered Laurel Matthews often found items for her interior decorating business at garage and yard sales, but this was a new experience for him. "I have a little money." Twenty dollars. Chump change to what he was used to spending. Surely, that could buy something at a yard sale. "Let's go."

"If we have to," Sam said.

At Mrs. Showalter's house, the kids ran to a table full of toys. Piles and stacks of stuff lay everywhere.

Henry didn't know where to start. He caught a glimpse of something white sitting on the grass and found a porch swing. The paint was peeling, but it looked sturdy. He checked the slats on the back. They were all there, and so were the chains to hang it with. The Wheelers' porch needed a swing.

Caitlin carried an old, naked baby doll in her arms. A sticker read twenty-five cents. "Can I have this?"

Ink marks covered the doll's arms and legs. A smiley-face sticker was plastered on the back of the doll's head. Talk about ugly. Not even a mother could love that hideous thing.

"Are you sure you want that doll?" he asked.

She cradled it against her chest. "I love my baby. Her name is Flower. Isn't she pretty?"

"Not as pretty as you, but you can have her."

"Thank you." Caitlin pointed at the swing. "What's that?"

"A swing for a porch."

"May I have this, please?" Abby held a science book, then noticed what they were discussing. "We used to have a porch swing. My mommy used to sit on it with us, and we'd wait for Daddy to come in from the fields."

"What happened to the swing?" Henry asked.

"It fell apart after our parents went to heaven," Abby said. "Elisabeth was so sad."

Elisabeth always seemed a little sad, even when she smiled. Henry would fix that. She needed more in her life than working, cooking, and cleaning. She needed happiness, love, and a porch swing. "Do you think she would like this?"

Abby nodded.

Sam walked up with a comic book. "Can I get this?"

Caitlin grinned. "Henry's buying a new porch swing."

"That doesn't look new to me." Sam frowned. "It's too old and beat up."

"That will make it cheaper to buy." Henry hoped the swing and the items the kids picked out were less than twenty dollars. He had his paycheck in his pocket, but he needed Elisabeth to cash it for him since he didn't have his cell phone nor his bank card. "We can fix the swing so it looks brand new."

Sam raised a brow. "Do you know how to do that?"

"No," Henry admitted. "But between all of us, we can figure it out and surprise Elisabeth with it."

The wariness in Sam's eyes reminded Henry of Elisabeth. "Why would you buy her a swing?"

"Because it might make her smile." He picked up the swing. "Let's see if we can afford all this."

They made their way to an older lady who the kids called Mrs. Showalter. Gray curls stuck out from the bright yellow bandanna she wore on her head. Big beaded earrings dangled from her ears. She wore a multicolored muumuu with large flowers on the fabric.

"How much is the porch swing, the doll, book, and comic?" Henry asked.

"We're going to paint the swing and give it to my sister," Caitlin added.

"That's thoughtful, dear." Mrs. Showalter added up the items on a small calculator. "Thirty dollars will cover everything."

Too much. Henry had never bargained before. This was his first time looking at a price tag. But he didn't want to disappoint the kids. "Fifteen."

Mrs. Showalter narrowed her brown eyes. "Twenty-five."

Still too high. He had one last shot. "Twenty."

She nodded once. "Sold."

The girls cheered. Sam mumbled, "Whatever," but he grabbed his comic.

Henry handed over his twenty.

"You drive a hard bargain, young man," Mrs. Showalter said.

Satisfaction flowed through him. He'd never felt so good buying gifts. "Thanks."

Mrs. Showalter smiled. "No, thank you."

The four of them stood around the newly purchased swing. Henry wasn't sure what to do with it. "Now we have to figure out how to get the swing back to the farm and refinish it without Elisabeth finding out."

Animation lit Sam's usually sullen face, and he pointed to an open gate. "Gabe will help us."

Gabe Logan pushed a wheelbarrow full of old bricks from what must be the backyard. He reminded Henry of a modern-day knight, except he used an electric drill instead of a sword for his rescues. "What have you got there?"

Sam pointed at the swing. "Can you tell us how to fix the porch swing Henry bought for Elisabeth?"

Mr. Fix-it Man set the wheelbarrow down and studied Henry. "You bought this for her?"

Henry nodded, wishing he'd watched a few of those home-improvement shows he'd glimpsed while channel surfing.

Gabe kneeled and checked out the swing as the girls gave him hugs. "It won't take long to get this back in shape. I'd be happy to help. Anything for my Bess."

His Bess? Gabe spoke with such affection, and his eyes softened.

Something clicked in Henry's mind. He didn't know anything about farms or building things or fixing machinery, but there was a man in Berry Patch who did. A man who wasn't wearing a wedding ring. A man who liked kids, too.

Gabe Logan might be the perfect man for Elisabeth and the Wheeler family.

Getting these two together would be easy for Henry to do. But the realization didn't bring any excitement or relief. Not the way playing matchmaker usually did. No, it only brought a sickening feeling in his stomach and the desire to swallow a handful of antacid tablets.

* * *

Two nights later, Henry wasn't feeling better. It wasn't his stomach this time, but insomnia. He couldn't sleep. He also couldn't move, thanks to Ruff and the nameless gray cat using Henry as a personal mattress. Henry would miss their companionship, but he wouldn't miss sharing a twin-size bed with them when he was gone. Maybe he could talk Dash or Blaise into getting a dog that Henry could visit and spoil. The other guys traveled or worked too much to have a pet, though Wes might consider it.

He wouldn't miss all the work it took to winterize the farm, either. At least he was no longer making so many mistakes. Or rather, not such noticeable ones.

He succeeded in playing fairy godfather. Well, sort of. His

efforts were working for everyone but Elisabeth. The kids loved their yard sale gifts, and the porch swing was coming along with Gabe's help.

Gabe.

Henry liked the man. Respected him, too. The guy was working miracles with the porch swing and teaching him a thing or two about carpentry. But woodworking wasn't the only thing Gabe knew about. He also knew women.

Forget fixing him up with Elisabeth.

Gabe Logan was too much like Henry—a rogue not a hero—and that wouldn't do for Elisabeth. She deserved better. She deserved the best.

But with Henry's job, he didn't have time to meet all the single men in Berry Patch and find the right one for Elisabeth. He would have to forgo matchmaking. The decision brought a rush of relief. He needed to put all his effort into not making mistakes around the farm, he rationalized.

Suddenly, the soft sounds of a trombone filled the air, followed by the plucking of strings and the crashing of cymbals... It sounded like an orchestra. But at this hour?

Henry scooted the gray cat from his chest and sat, careful not to bump his head on the upper bunk. He listened to the classical music. An odd sound, considering he'd never heard music being played at the Wheelers' house. Not from her cell phone and not on the radio.

The music piqued Henry's curiosity. Maybe Abby was analyzing a composer. Maybe there was more to Sam than baggy pants and a bad attitude. No, it had to be Abby.

Henry slid out of bed and headed downstairs. The only

lights were the dingy brass candlestick wall sconces above each end of the fireplace mantel. The soft glow provided enough light to see into the living room.

Halfway down the stairs, Henry froze.

Elisabeth sat on the couch. She wore a ratty light-colored robe. Her bare feet beat in time to the music. Her hair was loose and tousled.

He should go back to bed before she saw him, but then he did a double take.

Her eyes were closed. She had a serene Mona Lisa smile on her face. She swayed gently to the music. So lovely. He sat on the stairs and watched.

When a harp played its first note, so did Elisabeth. She plucked and strummed at a nonexistent harp with the skill and precision of a master. The play of emotions across her face captivated Henry. He'd never seen such passion, such concentration, such…contentment. Her expressions made him want to find a way to make her feel this way every single day, not just in the middle of the night, alone in the dark, air-harping.

This was a private moment he intruded on.

Henry didn't care. He would stay until she made him move. This new side of Elisabeth mesmerized him.

As the music continued to play, so did she. Not once did she open her eyes. She sat with such grace. Her elbows up and out, her thumbs up, and her fingers curved. Her feet pressed make-believe pedals. He wondered what she thought about, what she imagined as she played.

The song ended.

Elisabeth rose from the couch and bowed.

Henry clapped. A little too enthusiastically before he caught himself.

Too late.

The light on the end table next to her turned on.

Whoa. He'd forgotten about the clapper.

Elisabeth's eyelids sprang open. Her eyes sparkled. Her cheeks flushed. "What are you doing up?"

"I couldn't sleep." He climbed down the rest of the stairs. "I heard music and wanted to see what was going on."

"I'm sorry."

"Don't be sorry. It was worth getting up to see you play."

"I wasn't playing, only pretending." She sounded embarrassed.

"Or practicing?" he offered.

The color on her cheeks deepened. She sat on the couch.

He sat next to her. "I didn't know you were a musician."

"I'm not," she said quickly. "I mean, I used to be. But not any longer."

"You seem to enjoy it."

"It's okay." She clasped her hands together. "I started playing when I was six. An older woman in town asked my father if she could teach me. I think she felt sorry for us because my mother had died."

"Why did you stop playing?"

"No time. Plus, no reason to keep at it. Berry Patch doesn't have an orchestra. There are weddings and wineries, but it's easier to use a folk harp for those gigs. You could do it with a pedal harp, too, but it's not as easy to cart around."

Her answers sounded too rehearsed. Too much like excuses. Had she used them to justify not playing the harp? He would hate it if that were true.

"Where's your harp?" he asked.

A muscle clenched in her jaw. "I…I sold it."

"Why?"

"We needed the money." She sighed. "The Deere broke down right before harvest two years ago. The Suburban needed an overhaul. A hundred other things." The light in her eyes dimmed.

Henry wanted to bring it back. "Elisabeth—"

"It's no big deal. Really." She spoke quickly as if trying to convince herself. "It's not as if I was going to make a career out of playing the harp and travel the world performing with all the great orchestras."

"Was that your dream?"

"Yes. I mean, once it was." She tilted her chin. "Not now."

She might think so, but Henry wasn't convinced. "There's nothing wrong with dreams."

She shrugged.

He wanted to give her what she wanted. "You've given up so much of your life already to the farm and your siblings. You can't give up your dreams, too. It's not too late—"

"It is too late. I have the kids and the farm and my job."

"You could sell to Mr. Jackson."

"Never." Her eyes darkened. "This is the only home my family has ever known. I won't take that away from them. No matter what."

"Even if it's not what you want to do?"

"It's what I have to do. I don't deserve to have my dreams come true. If it weren't for me, my dad and stepmother would still be alive." The words tumbled out.

Her eyes widened once she realized what she'd revealed.

Henry needed to proceed slowly, cautiously. "I thought they were in a car accident."

"They were, but I'm the one who convinced them to go out on a date. If it weren't for me, they would still be alive. My brother and sisters would have parents. The farm wouldn't be struggling so badly. Neither would we."

"It isn't your fault, Elisabeth." Henry wanted to take away her pain—her guilt. "You weren't driving the car. You weren't even there. It was an accident."

She stared at the pictures on the mantel. "Caitlin wouldn't sleep through the night. I'd come home for the weekend, and my stepmother was so tired. She needed a break, so I told them to go on a date night, and I would watch the kids. They did, and they never came home again."

"They might have gone out anyway. Or had all the kids with them. Or a million other scenarios." Henry wanted to shake some sense into her. He knew what this kind of guilt could do to a person. "You can't continue blaming yourself."

Tears glimmered in her eyes. "How can I not blame myself?"

His heart ached for her.

He'd been there himself. Except he'd been a lot older than twenty-one, and he didn't have a baby to take care of and a brother and a sister and a farm. She would have had no time for herself. No time to mourn the loss of her parents. Only time to blame herself and give up her own life and dreams to make up for something that wasn't her fault.

"Things happen for no reason," he explained. "Sometimes good things, sometimes bad. And that can be hard to accept, especially when those things are beyond our control."

She said nothing. But her pain, her despair, tore at him.

He never opened up, never let anyone get too close, but just this once he needed to. For Elisabeth.

"After my parents were killed in the plane crash, I blamed myself." That wasn't easy for him to admit. He took a deep breath. "I was supposed to be on their flight, but I was too hungover and called them at the airport to tell them I would take a later flight. They were disappointed in me—a common occurrence—but said they would wait and take the later flight with me. I told them it wasn't necessary. I didn't relish being trapped on a transatlantic flight, listening to them tell me how I wasn't living up to their expectations. But if I hadn't been so selfish and let them wait for me, they wouldn't have been on that flight. They wouldn't have died."

Elisabeth's face lightened. "So you know."

"I know."

Her gaze met his. "How did you get through it?"

"I didn't at first. The guilt. The grief." Knowing he would never be able to gain his parents' love or show them they'd been wrong about him. "I spent my time partying. Until my friends stepped in. Laurel and Brett Matthews. Cynthia Sterling. Ryland Guyer. Wes Lockhart. A few other guys who Wes introduced me to. They got me through it. Saved me."

And Henry would do whatever it took to repay them for their friendship and ensure their happiness.

"You're lucky to have them," Elisabeth said. "I don't—didn't—have many friends to rely on. Theresa's great and always has been, but I was engaged when the accident happened, and my ex-fiancé didn't understand. He didn't even try."

"The guy must have been an idiot."

The corners of her mouth lifted. "That's what Theresa said. She's a good friend."

"Yes, she is. And smart." Henry held Elisabeth's hand. Engaged so young. Too young. No wonder it didn't last. And to have lost her parents, too. "Does Theresa think you were to blame?"

"No."

"Neither do I. So you're the only one we need to convince."

Her eyes darkened. "It's not going to happen."

"Try to accept it."

She sat silent. At least she hadn't said no.

That was a start. Henry would take it. "Say, 'I'm not to blame.'"

"I—I…" Tears fell from Elisabeth's eyes.

He covered her hand with his other one. "Try again."

She exhaled loudly. "I—I'm not to blame."

"Was that so hard?" he asked.

"Yes."

Henry released her hand, even though he wanted to keep touching her. "It gets easier."

"I doubt that."

He smiled to encourage her. "Keep saying it, and you'll see."

"I'll try." She rubbed her eyes. "I'm sorry for crying. I know guys hate tears."

Henry wanted to get her ex-fiancé alone in a small, dark room and make him cry. He put his arm around Elisabeth and gave her a squeeze. "Everyone needs a good cry. Even guys. And it's a lot cheaper than therapy."

"How do you do it?" She gazed up at him, and he felt as if he could lose himself in her eyes. "How can you make me feel so good when we're talking about something so serious?"

Warmth settled in the center of his chest. He found himself scooting toward her instead of away. "It's a gift."

"Thanks for sharing it with me."

Elisabeth hugged him. The fresh scent of her soap and shampoo filled his nostrils. He wanted to capture the fragrance in a bottle and spray it on his pillow. Her hair tickled his face, and he ached to run his fingers through the long, silky strands. She felt so soft and perfect in his arms.

Henry relished the shared moment. The hug. Her.

He yearned to kiss her.

With a pulse-pounding certainty, he knew he couldn't. He couldn't cross that line.

She didn't need his kisses; she needed his shoulder. A friend. He knew how to handle friends. He was good when it came to taking care of his friends and knowing what they needed.

Elisabeth released him.

A chill shivered through Henry, but her trusting smile reassured him. He had made the right choice. The only choice.

Henry caressed her cheek. "Anytime, Elisabeth. Anytime."

He meant it.

Chapter Twelve

"Kitty, kitty," Caitlin called. "Time to eat."

The fat gray cat didn't come, but Henry filled the stainless steel bowl with food anyway. The cat would be hungry sooner or later. It didn't look like it skipped any meals.

He was helping Caitlin with her chores while Elisabeth cooked dinner. Anything to keep him out of the kitchen and away from her.

Henry needed space.

He was getting too close to Elisabeth. Their midnight encounter two nights ago had only been the beginning. Working together, living together. He couldn't turn around without catching a glimpse of her. And if he didn't see Elisabeth, he was thinking about her. That didn't seem…right.

Not when he was only her friend.

Henry had to keep reminding himself of that. But it was

the truth. He was nothing more than the Wheelers' farmhand, friend, and fairy godfather. And when the time came to leave, he was out of there.

As Caitlin glanced around, she pouted. "Where is that cat?"

"Maybe if the cat had a name, he would come," Henry suggested.

"He has a name," she said. "Cat."

Henry chuckled. "I meant a name like Caitlin or Henry or Flower."

"How about Kitty?" she suggested.

"Good idea, but that name is a lot like Cat." Henry rubbed his chin. "How about Ritz?"

"I love Ritz crackers. So does Elisabeth."

He'd been thinking more along the lines of the Ritz-Carlton Hotel, but crackers worked. Especially if Elisabeth liked them—no. He shouldn't take her into account for everything. Not when he was only trying to be her friend, a temporary one at that. "Come, Ritz." As Caitlin called the new name, Henry shook the bowl of dry food as added incentive. "Dinnertime, Ritz."

The no-longer nameless cat came running as fast as his too-small-for-his-large-body legs could carry him.

Caitlin's mouth formed a perfect O. "Ritz likes his name."

"Yes, he does."

"I like you."

Henry ruffled her blond curls. "I like you, too, princess."

"Will you be my daddy?"

He froze. That wasn't what he expected her to say.

"Puh-lease?" she added.

Henry opened his mouth and then closed it. He was at a loss for words. Instinct told him to pack his duffel bag and leave. Forget about packing. He didn't need any of the stuff Cynthia had purchased for him.

Caitlin tugged on his hand. "Will you be my daddy, Henry?"

A ten-carat-diamond lump formed in his throat. He swallowed around it. "Do you want me to be the daddy if we play house?"

"Yes, but I also want you to be my daddy all the time. The other kids at my preschool have mommies and daddies. I just have Elisabeth. A sister. Abby's my sister, too." Caitlin scratched Ritz's head, and the cat purred as loud as a tractor engine. "All the princesses have daddies. Ariel, Jasmine, Belle, Aurora."

"What about Snow White and Cinderella?" Henry brushed aside his own question as two little lines formed above the bridge of Caitlin's nose. "You have a daddy."

"But he's in heaven. You're here with me."

Henry couldn't deny her four-year-old logic, but he had to be logical himself. He would never be good enough. He could never be the type of man someone would look up to and call Dad. Not only was he not father material, but he also didn't want to be a dad.

He was too selfish, too fond of his adventures and indulgences, and too determined to get his own way. His parents hadn't been the best role models, but Henry was pretty sure being a parent meant learning to give up control as much as it meant learning to take responsibility. And he wasn't good at either.

He winced. That made him sound like he had a Peter Pan complex. Well, he enjoyed some responsibilities, like making his friends happy. But being a father wasn't like making friends happy. Being a father didn't allow you to pick and choose when you showed up. If fathers made a mistake, it was a big deal.

If fathers made a mistake, it was a big deal.

Caitlin stared up at him expectantly.

He needed to say something to her, something a four-year-old would understand. "But I'm not a daddy. I'm…Henry."

Her lower lip quivered.

Oh man, he didn't want her to cry. She was just a little girl who wanted to be loved. He ignored the tug on his heart.

"What if I became your fairy godfather instead?" he asked.

Her cute nose crinkled. "What does a fairy godfather do?"

"He makes sure you're happy and smiling all the time."

She grinned. "You already do that. You bought me Flower and played vet with me. Oh, and remember when we colored?"

This was working. He smiled. "Then I'm one step ahead of the game."

"Will you still call me princess?"

"Of course, princess." He emphasized the last word. "Okay?"

As she nodded, her curls bobbed up and down. "Okay."

But it wasn't. Not really. Henry felt as if he'd dodged a bullet. Three of them. But Caitlin was happy, and he was relieved. He could be a fairy godfather or a real godfather.

A real father?

Forget it.

* * *

I'm not to blame.

Over the next few days, the words became Elisabeth's mantra. She was trying hard to believe them. The words gave her peace about her parents' deaths and a sense of freedom she hadn't thought possible. And it was all due to Henry.

Thinking about him brought a welcome smile to her face. She couldn't help it. He was thoughtful and hardworking. He'd stopped making so many mistakes and endangering the farm.

However, he was also becoming a…problem.

She glanced at the clock on her dashboard and stepped on the accelerator. The engine spurted. She pressed on the gas pedal again. Finally, the Suburban sped up.

She couldn't deny Henry was gorgeous. Any breathing female would be attracted to him. But Elisabeth's growing feelings for him went beyond the physical, and that bothered her. A lot. She'd lost a fiancé over having to raise her siblings and had no regrets. Keeping them all together was the right choice. She would never get involved with a man who didn't want kids. Not that she wanted to get involved with Henry.

She didn't.

Except she was getting attached. So were the kids. She didn't want to think about what would happen when Henry left, but she had to.

He would be leaving. Just as soon as Manny returned or once Henry's month was up in a little over two weeks. Elisabeth didn't know what would happen first, but it didn't matter. The result would be the same.

She had to prepare herself and the kids for his departure. They would have to get used to an empty space at the table again. They would have to give Ruff extra love and attention. Ritz would be back to sleeping on top of her. They would have to put a radio in the bathroom to replace Henry's singing in the shower.

Thinking about all those things made her heart hurt.

That was bad.

Maybe it would be smart to distance herself and the kids from Henry. But how?

Caitlin tagged along after Henry as much as Ruff did. Abby sought him out to help her with homework or some advanced subject she'd decided to study for fun. Sam pretended not to care, but Elisabeth noticed he watched Henry and not with the same mistrust he used to show. She even looked forward to having coffee with him during their breaks.

Distance wasn't possible.

Elisabeth stopped the car in front of the barn. She jerked the parking brake into place, yanked the keys out of the ignition, and jumped out of the Suburban. If she hurried, she could get the feed unloaded and a chicken in the Crock-Pot for dinner.

Ruff barked.

"Home from work?" Henry asked from behind her.

The rich sound of his voice sent a shiver of pleasure along her spine. *Ugh.* She didn't want to react to his voice. To him. Not when she already missed him, and he wasn't even gone. Elisabeth pushed a strand of hair that had fallen out of her ponytail behind her ear. "Yes."

"A little early for you."

It wasn't a question. Elisabeth hadn't known Henry paid attention to her schedule. His interest flattered her. Made her feel warm and tingly inside.

Stop.

What he said to her shouldn't mean anything. that him noticing something small about her life made her feel this way.

Elisabeth opened the tailgate to remove the two fifty-pound bags of feed.

She untied her stained apron from work and tossed it into the SUV. Bill Tucker's two-year-old son had squirted a bottle of ketchup all over the table and her, but she didn't want the fabric to get dirtier. "A coworker is sick, so Kathy needs me to work the dinner shift, too. I just have to do a few things here first."

"That'll be a long day for you."

She struggled to pull one of the feed bags out. "I've done it before."

"Let me take that."

Elisabeth appreciated his offer, but she didn't need the

help. She wouldn't rely on him any more than she had to. "Thanks, but I can do it."

"I know you can." Henry picked up the bag without any effort. "I want to help."

She worked on removing the next one.

"Do you want me to get the kids from school and watch them for you?" he asked.

Babysitting was a long way from wanting to have children of his own, but his offer made her wonder if the kids were softening his views on having a family. "Theresa's doing it. She already picked up Caitlin from preschool and will get Sam and Abby later, but thanks."

"I'll do it some other time."

Her heart danced at the possibility. "Sure."

"What about this weekend? I can watch them, and you can go out."

"Out where?" she asked.

"Out on a date."

Huh? Elisabeth nearly dropped the bag, but thankfully, Henry grabbed it. She was so flustered she couldn't even thank him. All she could think about was him offering to babysit so she could go out with another man.

Ouch. She needed more than distance from Henry; she needed a reality check.

"I don't date." *Ick.* She sounded like a pathetic, shriveled-up spinster. Might as well hand him a list with all her flaws and fears. "I mean, I rarely date. The kids and all. Theresa always wants to fix me up with someone, but I hate blind dates as much as I hate people playing matchmaker with me."

Henry stared at her. "So, you're not looking for Mr. Right?"

"I'm not looking for Mr. Anything." But as she said the words, she got the funny feeling she was looking at Mr. Right himself. Her mouth went dry.

"Instead of a date, you and Theresa could hit the town for a girls' night out."

"We haven't done that in a long time." Too long, Elisabeth realized.

"You could have fun."

"Why are you so interested in me having fun?"

Henry widened his stance. "You work harder than anyone I know. You need a break, if only for a few hours. Away from the bistro, the farm, and the kids."

"Three kids can be a lot of work. Think you can handle them?"

"Yes." Confidence laced the word. "Caitlin goes to bed early. Abby likes to read. Sam and I can figure something out or just talk."

Elisabeth raised a brow. "Talk to Sam?"

"Or look through his comic books."

Henry did know the kids pretty well. He was good with them. As long as cooking wasn't involved, she wouldn't worry about their safety. Not with Sam there. Abby was mature for her age. Caitlin would describe everything to Elisabeth, down to the smallest detail the next morning. Maybe this could work. And she did need time away. Not from the farm or the kids. But from Henry. "I'll talk to Theresa."

"Do," Henry encouraged. "Ask her about this Friday night."

"I will." Her feet dragged on the way to the house, and she glanced back. The way he was looking at her made her heart beat triple time. "And, Henry…thank you."

A dazzling smile lit up his face. "My pleasure."

Great. He was pleased because she had agreed to go out for a night. Without him. She'd wanted some distance, and she'd gotten it. So why wasn't she just as happy about it?

* * *

Friday—girls' night out—arrived. Henry was prepared. Elisabeth had cashed his second paycheck for him that morning. He'd spent his entire first check on supplies for the nearly finished porch swing and a few extra treats for Elisabeth, but this week, he had money left over after shopping for tonight's activities—a tea party for Caitlin, a build-your-own ice cream sundae science experiment for Abby, and a rented video game system for Sam.

Almost time.

Henry was itching to get started. He rubbed his palms together.

The Wheelers' fairy godfather had found his groove.

It was all he could do not to write out an itinerary for Elisabeth and Theresa's girls' night out. Doing so would be overstepping his bounds, but he felt odd not being able to ensure she would have a good time.

Elisabeth walked down the stairs. "How do I look?"

Henry's breath caught in his throat. He was used to seeing her wearing jeans or her server uniform or a Sunday church dress or her bathrobe. But all dressed up…

Whoa. She cleaned up well.

Her powder-blue button-down shirt matched her eyes. Her above-the-knee khaki skirt made her legs look longer. Good thing he'd decided not to play matchmaker. She didn't need one. What she needed was a bodyguard. Henry swallowed. Hard.

"You're stunning." He forced the words from his dry throat.

Elisabeth glanced at the brown mules on her feet, and her cheeks reddened. "Thanks."

"You're wearing makeup."

She touched her cheek. "Is it too much?"

"No, it's just right. And your hair, too," he said. "The men of Berry Patch had better watch out."

Her sparkling gaze met his. "You're so sweet."

She wouldn't think he was so sweet if she had any clue how attractive he found her.

A car door slammed. Time to pull himself together. Not only for his sake but for the kids' sake, too.

"You and Theresa have fun tonight," he said.

Elisabeth picked up her sweater from the back of the couch. "Oh, Theresa couldn't make it."

"Then who—"

A knock sounded. Henry opened the front door and wanted to slam it shut.

Gabe Logan stood wearing a wide grin and holding a colorful bouquet. "How's it going, Henry?"

Chapter Thirteen

The scents of basil and garlic lingered in the restaurant's air, where Elisabeth sat across from Gabe at the cozy table for two. Dinner was a set three course menu..

She glanced around at the decor, which she would describe as farmhouse chic with flickering votives and rose buds in eclectic glass jars. Cynthia Sterling would fit right in here. So would Henry. Well, the way he'd been dressed the first time she met him.

Elisabeth, however, felt like an underdressed fraud. This place was too nice, too romantic, and too expensive for a night out with her best friend's big brother, who was just being nice by filling in for Theresa.

Gabe leaned back in his chair. "What do you think?"

She took a sip of water, hoping to soothe her dry throat. "I thought we'd eat in Berry Patch."

"Did you really think I'm the kind of guy who would take you out to the place you work?"

Yes, but she wouldn't admit that, especially since he'd taken so much care tonight. Gabe wore a button-down shirt with a pair of brown pants, not his typical T-shirt and jeans no matter the weather. His hair had been recently trimmed, and his usual five o'clock shadow was nowhere in sight, so he'd shaved before picking her up.

He'd obviously put in some effort for her, which Elisabeth appreciated. "Well, you got pushed into taking me out tonight after your sister had to cancel."

He shook his head. "Not pushed. I volunteered."

That…surprised Elisabeth. She leaned forward. "Really?"

"I could be home with my dog or here with you. Easy decision."

She wasn't sure if that was a well-practiced line or sincere, but she would go with the latter. "Well, thanks. I don't get out much, so this is more than I expected."

"You should expect more, Bess. So much more. Not everyone is like that stupid college boy you brought home."

She laughed. Henry had called Toby an idiot. Both he and Gabe were right. "I hope no one else I meet is like him."

"Me too." Gabe motioned to her glass of red wine and picked up his. "A toast."

She grabbed the wineglass stem. "To?"

He grinned, the corners of his eyes crinkling, making him even more attractive. "You."

The guy was handsome, but then again so was Henry. Nope. She needed to stop thinking about him when she was out with someone else. Even if Gabe wasn't a real date. "I have to hear this."

"Oh no. The pressure." Gabe cleared his throat. "To Bess, the girl who grew up to be an amazing woman, friend, sister, server, berry farmer, and dinner companion."

The words brought a rush of heat up her neck. "That's so sweet."

He winked. "All true."

"Thank you."

As his gaze met Elisabeth's, he tapped his glass to hers. "Cheers."

She took a small sip, lowered her glass, and stared at the wine bottle. The label was from a local winery. "Delicious pinot noir."

"It is." Gabe studied her. "What's on your mind?"

Elisabeth looked at him. "What makes you think something's on my mind?"

He smiled. "I've known you since you were in kindergarten."

Okay, he had her there. In some ways, Gabe reminded her of Henry. Both men were attractive and knew the right things to say. Her farmhand was only there temporarily, and Gabe didn't want to settle down, no matter how charming he might act. Both men were off-limits. Yet sometimes it was easy to think maybe they didn't know what they wanted.

Now she was just being silly. "I just wasn't expecting to go out to a nice place. No offense, but takeout pizza is about as fancy as we get at the farm."

"None taken, but I meant what I said about all you do. Theresa suggested a few things we could try, but I've heard a few clients talk about this place. Figured this was the perfect night to see if it's as good as they all say. So you're helping me out here. Now, if it turns out badly…"

"It won't. I'm already impressed."

"Then I have nothing to worry about." He took another sip of wine. "How's Henry working out? Any more bee incidents?"

"Luckily, no. But the goats might be out to get him."

"Poor guy, but he's right about you needing some time away from the kids and the farm."

She glanced around at the full tables of adults having soft conversations. "I guess I do."

"No guess about it. And I have the entire night planned out."

"You mean there's more than this place?"

His eyes filled with mischief. "Yes, but it's a surprise."

"It'll still be a surprise if you tell me now."

"I see where Abby gets her cleverness from."

Elisabeth's cheeks heated. Gabe had a reputation of being a ladies' man, but she'd never seen him in action until tonight. "If you think compliments will get you anywhere—"

"As long as they keep making you blush, I'll keep saying them. And every word is sincere."

She had no idea how to respond, so she took a small sip of wine. But she was struck by how much she couldn't stop thinking about Henry. Something told her he would be very similar to Gabe if they went out on a date. Except that would never happen.

Elisabeth wanted to shake her farmhand out of her head. She smiled at Gabe. "What remodeling projects are you working on right now?"

* * *

Babysitting was going well. The tea party had been a success as well as the ice cream sundae experiments. He'd played house with the girls and handled being "Daddy" without suffering an anxiety attack or needing to call a therapist.

Caitlin had fallen asleep on the couch at eight o'clock. Abby at nine. Both were tucked safely in their beds. Henry had checked on them twice. Now, Ruff slept at his feet while Henry sat on the couch. Ritz was curled up on the recliner. All Henry needed now was for Elisabeth to get home.

"Yes." Sam raised his hands in the air. "I win."

"Not again." Henry tossed his controller on the coffee table and glanced at the clock: 10:06 p.m. Only eight minutes had passed since the last time he'd looked.

Why wasn't Elisabeth home yet? Dinner didn't take that long. And there wasn't much nightlife in Berry Patch.

"Why do you keep checking the clock?" Sam asked.

"Wondering when your sister might be home."

"Don't worry about her." Sam stuck a new game into the video game console. "She's with Gabe. He'll take care of her."

That was what Henry was afraid of. Knowing Gabe Logan's reputation, he could find plenty of ways to entertain Elisabeth.

Henry wrung his hands.

Sam sat next to him. "Are you ready to play the snowboarding game?"

Anticipation filled his voice. Sam wasn't so bad once you got past the apathy and the sneer and his being eleven. His vocabulary even included other words besides "whatever" and "sucks." Not to mention, he had amazing hand-eye coordination. Henry needed something to take his mind off Elisabeth. Maybe a different game would do the trick. "Sure, but I've never played that one."

"It's not hard," Sam said. "Even you should be able to figure it out."

"Even me?"

The corners of Sam's mouth edged up.

Henry picked up his controller and readied himself like a sharpshooter from the Old West. "I'll show you."

By the time midnight rolled around, Sam was asleep in bed. Henry had played enough video games to give him carpal tunnel syndrome, and Elisabeth still wasn't home.

He didn't like it.

He didn't like the way he kept glancing at the clock.

He didn't like the way he wanted to call the police station and make sure there hadn't been an accident.

She was his friend. His boss. That was why he was concerned about her. There wasn't any other reason. Henry picked up toys and put them in the basket. He wasn't much of a housekeeper, but he had to do something to keep himself from imagining Elisabeth lying on the side of the road or kissing Gabe in the front seat of his truck.

Don't think about either of those things.

Henry carried the popcorn bowl into the kitchen, dumped the half-popped kernels into the garbage, and washed the bowl.

Why hadn't he been the one to go out with her? He could show her a better time than Gabriel Logan.

The answer hit Henry: Sam, Abby, and Caitlin. If Henry hadn't suggested that Elisabeth go out, she would be home.

With him.

Henry tossed the dish towel on the counter. He only had himself to blame.

He returned to the living room and plopped onto the couch.

Headlights shone through the front window, and then a vehicle pulled to a stop outside.

A two-ton weight fell off Henry's shoulders. Now, if he could just see her.

Henry watched the clock. A minute passed. And another. Yet another. The seconds dragged on. Each minute seemed like an hour.

What was going on outside?

It didn't take that long to say good night. Unless…

Henry sprang to his feet. He was halfway to the door when it opened, and Elisabeth stepped inside.

"What's going on?" she asked.

"I, uh, was going to let Ritz out."

She hung her purse on a hook by the door. "He has a cat door."

"I forgot."

Henry studied her. The circles under her eyes were less noticeable. The rosy glow on her cheeks made her look younger. She was smiling and radiant. Telling her to go out had been the right thing, even if her date was with Gabe.

"How were the kids?" she asked.

"Great."

She arched a brow. "Even Sam?"

"Especially Sam. He enjoyed the game system I rented. We played after the girls went to bed."

"I wasn't sure about you renting that, but it was thoughtful of you to get something Sam would enjoy."

"He did and beat me badly," Henry admitted ruefully. "How was your date?"

His jaw clenched. He hadn't meant to ask, but he was…curious. He sat on the couch.

"It wasn't really a date."

Good news. Great, actually. Though he realized whatever she called tonight shouldn't have mattered. "What did you do?"

"We drove to Dundee for dinner. It was a great place neither of us had ever been to. The food was delicious. Then we went to The Vine to hear a new band. They were good but loud." She sat next to Henry. "The evening was nice. Gabe treated me like a princess."

Henry's hands clenched. "You deserve to be treated like a princess."

By me. Not him.

"Did he kiss you?" The words rushed out before Henry could stop them.

"Gabe kisses everyone."

So did Henry. That was a red flag.

His gut told him Gabe Logan was not the man for Elisabeth. Henry had already decided not to play matchmaker, so finding someone else wasn't an option. What else could he do? He rubbed his chin.

"You okay?" she asked.

"Fine. I'm just fine."

"Me, too." Her smile reached her eyes. "Thanks for suggesting I go out. I needed it more than I realized."

"I'm happy you had fun." But he wasn't happy. Not really. And that bugged him. He was her friend, her fairy godfather, and he should be happy she'd enjoyed herself. She had needed tonight. She needed more. *And if it turns out she needs Gabe—*

She leaned forward and kissed Henry. On the lips. Hard.

She tasted like wine and chocolate. His heart slammed against his chest.

Wanting this kiss was wrong. He didn't care. Because it felt right. And he wanted more of her kisses and more of her.

He was crossing the line and had jumped without a thought. But she'd been the one to initiate the kiss. Not him. This was her doing. Not his.

And he enjoyed kissing her. A lot.

Still, he held back. Somehow, he managed not to touch her anywhere except on the lips. It wasn't nearly enough, but that was all he dared.

Achingly, the kiss came to an end.

A slow smile spread over her face. "I thought so."

He could barely breathe, let alone think. "Thought what?"

"That you kiss better than Gabe." She rose from the couch. "Good night, Henry."

He sat there, stunned.

There was nothing good about tonight.

Henry had left the evening up to fate, but Elisabeth had grabbed the reins.

The result? Chaos.

She'd turned everything upside down by looking so gorgeous. By going out with the flower-toting Gabe and kissing him. And by ending the night kissing Henry.

He wanted to be in control but didn't want to take responsibility. Tonight proved he couldn't control Elisabeth, yet he couldn't help feeling responsible for her, either.

Henry didn't like it.

He was supposed to be her fairy godfather, but that was the last thing he felt like right now.

All he wanted to do was take her in his arms and kiss her. He wanted to shower her with diamonds and pearls and sapphires. He wanted to show her how wonderful life could be if she didn't have the responsibilities of the farm and her siblings.

But his wanting those things made no sense.

Henry wasn't there for the long haul. He didn't believe in the long haul. He wasn't the man she thought he was. He wasn't even close. He would never be good enough for her. He would never be the type of man she loved. No, not loved. Wanted.

And that hurt. More than he thought possible.

Chapter Fourteen

The following afternoon, Elisabeth sat in the passenger seat of Theresa's car, staring out the window at the passing scenery. Early morning chores, a car that wouldn't start, and the busy Saturday lunch shift at the bistro had worn her out. Not to mention a restless night.

She had dreamed Henry was staying on the farm. Not just until Manny returned but forever. In her dream, she'd been euphoric at the news.

Too bad her life didn't have room for fantasies, daydreams, and romance. Her shoulders sagged.

"You okay?" Theresa asked.

"I will be. Nothing a hot shower and a nap can't fix." Elisabeth straightened. "Thanks for the ride home. I hope Gabe fixed the Suburban."

"He was working on it when I left to pick you up. If it

can be fixed, he'll do it, but the Suburban is almost as old as you are. You need a new car."

What she really needed was a new brain.

No wonder she dreamed about Henry after the way she'd kissed him last night. Kissing him the first time had been bad enough, but twice? She couldn't even blame it on the wine; she'd had one glass at dinner and half a glass while listening to the band.

The fault lay entirely with her.

She'd kissed him only to prove to herself she'd magnified his kiss to mythic proportions because she hadn't been kissed in such a long time. After Gabe's pleasant good-night kiss with no zings or tingles or fireworks, Elisabeth had figured Henry's kiss would be the same—nice but uneventful. She would be able to distance herself mentally and forget about his kisses and him.

She'd been wrong. He hadn't even taken her in his arms, but his lips against hers were all she needed to realize she hadn't blown his kiss out of proportion. To be honest, kissing him had been better than she remembered. Much better.

Elisabeth leaned her head back against the seat. "I need a new everything."

Theresa turned on her playlist, and a romantic ballad played over the car speakers. "Does that include a new farmhand?"

"Henry's doing better." If only he was as great at farming as he was at kissing, they could turn the farm around. "He's not making as many mistakes. Though the other day when I asked him to bring a chicken for dinner, he thought he had to kill one." Her insides had melted when she saw him holding on to a hen and petting it, an ax on the ground outside the chicken coop. "Luckily, he couldn't do it. He was so relieved when I showed him the freezer where we kept the frozen chicken."

"Henry's a great guy," Theresa said.

"How would you know?"

"You haven't been complaining about him. You haven't really talked about Henry at all." Theresa glanced over at her. "What's up with that?"

"Nothing."

"You like him."

Like didn't describe how Elisabeth felt about Henry. She wasn't sure what word did. "He works for me."

"That's an excuse, not a reason." Theresa tapped the steering wheel to the beat of the music. "If you don't like him, why are you blushing?"

"I'm…I'm hot."

"And bothered?"

Elisabeth wasn't about to answer that.

Theresa continued. "I don't blame you for feeling that way. He's perfect for you."

"I thought *you* liked him."

She shrugged. "I would never stand in the way of true love."

"True what?"

"Love." Theresa winked. "Elisabeth plus Henry equals true love."

If only…no, Elisabeth couldn't think about that. "You'll only be disappointed if you think that's true."

"Dinner," Elisabeth answered as she stood in front of the stove and stirred one of the pots.

"Liver and onions," Abby added as if she had to eat mud for dinner.

Caitlin pouted. "I'm not eating it."

"Me either," Sam said.

"You'll eat it." Elisabeth placed full plates in front of each of them. "It's good for you."

Henry had never seen something so unappetizing in all his life. Pâté was made from liver, but this? No way could this dish be good for anyone. "I'm not that hungry."

"I'm not hungry," Sam echoed.

Elisabeth sat. "Children who are starving all over the world would be happy to eat this."

"Let's FedEx it to them," Abby murmured. "I'd rather starve. A person can survive without food. Water, however, is critical."

Henry bit back a chuckle. Abby was so precocious and adorable. He wondered what she would be when she grew up. A scientist, a doctor, a CEO?

"It's not that bad," Elisabeth said.

As she took a bite, he glimpsed a slight grimace as she chewed.

"Do you actually like this?" he asked.

She drank half her glass of milk. "My stepmother used to make it."

He noticed she didn't answer his question. Finally, something he didn't like about her—the way she prepared liver and onions. Not that he would like it prepared the other way, but he refused to think about that.

Sam slumped. "I didn't like it when Mom made it, and hers was better."

Elisabeth drew her lips into a thin line. "Just eat."

Not one of the kids picked up a fork. Henry had always felt the need to support Elisabeth, but not in this instance. Backing her up would be something a father would do. Taking the "mother's" side. He didn't want to give the kids the wrong impression. Especially Caitlin. Besides, it would be hypocritical of him when he wasn't about to eat the dinner either.

"Ruff wouldn't eat this," Sam said.

Elisabeth sighed. "Yes, he would."

"Why don't we find out?" Henry suggested. They all needed to have more fun, especially Elisabeth. And if Ruff kept them from having to eat the meal, that would be a bonus. "We can do an experiment like we read about in your science book, Abby."

Elisabeth frowned. "We're not going to waste good food."

"We aren't," Sam muttered.

Abby tilted her head. "Dogs aren't supposed to eat onions."

Henry didn't know that. "We'll remove them."

"Ruff isn't going to any of it," Sam added.

"What's our hypothesis?" Henry asked.

"That Ruff will not eat the liver," Abby said.

"Good," Henry said. "Our assumptions?"

"Ruff has taste buds," Abby offered.

"The food is inedible," Sam said.

Elisabeth said nothing, but her eyes were watchful.

"I will perform the experiment." Henry scooped up a small piece of liver with his fork, wiped off the meat with his napkin to make sure no onions were included, and placed the bite-sized piece on the floor. "Come here, boy."

Ruff trotted over. He sniffed the meat and gobbled it down.

Elisabeth tilted her chin. "Told you so."

"What are the conclusions, Abby?" Henry asked.

"We have disproved our hypothesis and one of our assumptions," Abby explained. "Ruff does not have any taste buds."

Sam grinned. "Good one, sis."

Abby beamed.

"She's convinced me," Elisabeth capitulated. "You don't have to eat it."

The kids cheered. Henry fought the urge to join them, but he didn't want to be rude and hurt Elisabeth's feelings.

A smile tugged at the corners of her mouth. "So, what should we do now?"

"Food fight?" Henry suggested.

The kids leaned over the table toward Elisabeth. Their eyes widened with anticipation.

"No." It was only one word, but her tone said it all. "Before you complain, what about dinner at the Burger Basket? Gabe said the Suburban was as good as new. We can find out if he's right."

"Burger Basket is almost as good as a food fight," Sam said.

"I want a chocolate milkshake," Caitlin said.

"This will ruin our budget," Abby added.

"No, it won't." Henry pulled out Elisabeth's chair for her. "Dinner is my treat."

She looked at him. "You don't have to take us out."

Henry didn't. He wasn't her husband or their father or anybody's provider, but he was their friend. He wanted to do this for them—for her.

It was only dinner at the Burger Basket, not The French Laundry in the Napa Valley.

He was, after all, their fairy godfather. "I want to."

"Then you have first dibs on the swing tonight," Elisabeth said.

As long as he could have it all to himself. Because if he sat on the swing with her, if he stared long enough into her caring blue eyes, he might see a reflection of the man she wanted. The man he could never be.

* * *

Sitting on the porch swing, Elisabeth gazed at the millions of stars twinkling in the night sky and smiled. The lack of city lights on the farm made for the best stargazing. It was an absolutely perfect evening. Everything about today had been excellent too. Satisfaction overflowed to the tips of her toes.

The Suburban ran perfectly, her porch had been transformed into a thing of beauty, dinner out with milkshakes had been great, and the game of charades after they arrived home had been so much fun. The kids seemed happier, especially Sam. Elisabeth knew the reason.

Henry.

He was becoming more than just their farmhand; he was becoming a part of their family. She pictured him in her mind, and her pulse skittered. She inhaled sharply.

The realization should have scared her more than it did, especially since Manny had left a message while they were out to dinner, saying he hoped to return soon. But until *soon* arrived, Henry was still here. And that made her happy.

So, so happy.

A door shut somewhere off in the distance, and she glanced in the direction of the barn, which had the only other doors besides the house and chicken coop. It was dark, so she squinted to get a better view.

Henry walked to the house with Ruff tagging along at his side. His stride exuded confidence and strength, and it was all she could do not to sigh.

Oh, she had it bad, but she couldn't help herself.

Each time Elisabeth saw Henry, his pull was stronger. She wanted to fight the temptation to be drawn in. That was what she should be doing.

But not tonight.

Tonight, she wanted the magic of today to continue. Just this once, she wanted to forget her responsibilities and fears.

Elisabeth combed her fingers through her hair in a nervous habit, but she didn't care. Henry had made her feel carefree and young today. Two ways she never thought she'd ever feel again. He'd gone to so much trouble for her, and she would never forget his thoughtfulness. She ran her palm along the swing.

"Having fun?" Henry asked.

"Yes."

She kicked her feet out in front of her the way she had when she was a little girl. As a child, she'd believed in knights in shining armor, the same way her sisters did now. But she'd had to grow up fast and let go of girlish fantasies. After Toby had proved he wasn't Prince Charming, she stopped believing in happy endings altogether.

Maybe that had been the wrong thing to do. Maybe those things existed. Maybe Henry… "I know you had dibs on the swing tonight, but I'm hoping you won't mind sharing."

A muscle twitched in his neck. He didn't move.

With an encouraging smile, she patted the space next to her. "There's plenty of room for both of us."

Henry obliged, leaving space between them. As she glanced at the bench where they sat, the pit of her stomach tingled. She fought the urge to inch closer to him. Did she dare?

Elisabeth couldn't deny attraction had been building between her and Henry since he arrived, but since it had nowhere to go, she figured she couldn't be hurt by it.

"Where are the kids?" he asked.

"In bed," she said. "You and Gabe wore them out working on this beautiful porch."

"I'm happy you like it."

"I love it." She sighed, feeling happier than she had in so long. "Today has been such a great day."

"I hope it's the first of many."

"I don't think that's possible."

He stared at her, and more tingles formed in her stomach. "Anything is possible."

"I hope so," she said wistfully. If he stayed…

"I know so."

She didn't know what he meant by that, and she was afraid to ask in case his answer spoiled the mood.

Silence surrounded them. She waited for it to become uncomfortable, but that didn't happen. The quiet seemed natural, welcoming, and soothing.

Henry shifted on the swing. "The only thing missing is music."

"And dancing."

He nodded.

"You know, a little music would be a nice way to end the night." She bit her lip. "Would you please sing that song you always sing in the shower?"

He drew his brows together. "I didn't know you could hear me."

"Only sometimes." She liked how he seemed a little embarrassed. She didn't feel so vulnerable when he was, too. "The kids don't like it when they can't hear you."

His smile reached all the way to his eyes, giving her the good kind of chills. "I'll make sure I sing loud enough for my audience from now on."

"That'll make them happy."

His gaze captured hers. "And you?"

A kiss would make her happier. "And me, too."

A beat passed. Then another. A guarded expression crossed his face, and his eyes darkened. Slowly, he rose and extended his arm. "May I have this dance?"

"Dance?"

He motioned to the yard. "Underneath the stars."

So romantic. Her pulse sped up. She wanted this, but a part of her was worried about letting herself get too carried away. Henry would be leaving, logic reminded.

But he was here now, her heart countered.

"What about music?" she asked.

"You asked me to sing." He bowed. "Your wish is my command."

Excitement rippled through her, washing away her reluctance. It was only a dance, and she'd wished to let go of real life for one night. Elisabeth took hold of Henry's hand.

He led her down the porch stairs to the front yard and placed his other hand on her waist. As he sang "What a Wonderful World," they danced. He wasn't Louis Armstrong, but Henry's voice sent shivery tingles down her spine that joined the ones already in her stomach.

Believing the words he sang wasn't hard to do. Everything seemed wonderful tonight. The stars, the moonlight, Henry. This was the stuff dreams were made of. How could she ever thank him?

A kiss?

Too bad the kiss she had in mind wouldn't be one of gratitude. She looked away from his lips.

He finished the song but didn't release her. They continued to dance, even though their only music was the chirping of crickets. The tenderness of his gaze made her knees wobble. She was glad he held her, or she might have stumbled.

But if she fell, she had the feeling Henry would catch her. That filled her with optimism. She wanted to take the chance and open herself up to the possibilities.

Maybe he was different. Maybe, despite his words, he would want them all. Maybe when Manny returned, Henry wouldn't want to leave.

He stopped dancing and released her.

"Thank you." Her voice sounded husky, and she cleared her throat. "Today— This— It's all been…wonderful."

He caressed her cheek with his calloused fingers. "You're the one who is wonderful."

She waited for him to kiss her. A kiss was what she wanted.

What she needed.

Her heart pounded so loudly she was sure he could hear it.

From the corner of her eye, she glimpsed a falling star shooting across the sky like a firework.

I wish Henry would stay.

She hadn't had time to think before the wish had popped into her mind.

Why hadn't she wished for a kiss? A wish that had a chance of coming true? Elisabeth sucked in a breath.

"It's late." Henry took a step back. The distance seemed larger than the space separating them. "You have church in the morning."

That was still hours away. But she could see in the depths of his eyes she wouldn't get the kiss she wanted so badly.

Something had changed. The real world had crept back in. He'd felt it, and so had she.

This wasn't some enchanted evening. Henry wasn't a knight who would remain by her side forever. Dreams didn't come true. That was the truth she'd forgotten tonight. Well, not forgotten, but she pretended it wasn't the case.

Disappointment ricocheted through her, but her shoulders didn't sag. She stood tall with her chin raised.

At least she'd tasted a little magic today and tonight. That was more than she'd had in the past four years. Better than nothing, right?

She glanced at Henry.

Wasn't it?

Chapter Fifteen

The days and nights turned into another week. One more week of backbreaking farm work. One more week of bringing smiles to the Wheelers' faces. One more week of having more fun than Henry thought possible.

Who could have thought taking on the responsibilities of this farm and this family could make him…

Not happy, Henry thought, panicked. He was not a responsible kind of guy, but he took satisfaction in knowing he hadn't screwed up too badly.

Yet.

Henry stood on the bank of the river with Elisabeth, where water for the irrigation system was drawn. The Willamette Valley skies had darkened to an ominous gray, and rain fell. The weather matched the storm raging inside him.

The line between Henry the fairy godfather and Henry

the man blurred. He wanted to blame Elisabeth, but she couldn't help being so open and honest and nurturing. Not to mention beautiful. He'd had the urge to kiss her so badly the night they'd danced beneath the stars in the front yard. But he'd been trying to fulfill her wish, not his own.

Henry had to remind himself of that whenever they were alone. Like now. He tried keeping their interactions light, friendly, and completely nonphysical. No touching, no swinging on the porch together, nothing to put himself near her. It hadn't been easy, not when he thought about her each night before bed and every morning when he woke up.

He also felt himself growing attached to the kids. Sam, Abby, and Caitlin had become happy, delightful children who were a pleasure to be around. Laughter had become as contagious as smiles this past week as they made Halloween costumes. That was exactly what Henry had hoped to accomplish.

But there was a problem.

He was beginning to want to be a Wheeler himself.

He no longer minded living on the farm. Sleeping in was a luxury he could live without. Eating out wasn't as good as staying in for a home-cooked meal. Using his credit card wasn't as rewarding as spending hard-earned cash. He didn't even miss champagne all that much. Though he still hated having to clean up after himself.

It didn't take an IQ the size of Abby's to realize he was in over his head—way over and about to drown if he wasn't careful. Leaving the farm was the best option, but Manny hadn't returned yet. Henry couldn't leave Elisabeth and the kids alone.

He wasn't about to shirk his responsibility.

This was the one time he wouldn't pack up and hop on his private jet as usual.

Down at the river, Elisabeth pointed out the irrigation equipment they needed to pull out. "I can't believe I didn't remove the irrigation pump before Manny left. But we need to do it today. See the electrical wiring up there? A heavy rain could cause the water to swell, which would ruin the electrical system, and we'd need to replace it."

That would cost money they didn't have, and it was already raining hard. They'd better get to work. Henry adjusted his gloves.

The Wheelers were barely scraping by. He didn't see any way for Elisabeth's life to improve if she continued with the berry farm. Farming was a lose-lose situation, with prices set for harvests, payments from canneries spread out over months, and intense competition from foreign produce importers. The fact he'd learned that stuff in the past couple of weeks blew him away as did watching Elisabeth refuse to give up despite the odds.

Not even money would help make a difference. Sure, money would make the family more comfortable and less dependent on the land, but nothing would change the weather or the crop yields or the other uncertainties she faced every single day working on the farm. There was no control. No stability. Only responsibility. He hated that and wanted no part of it. But he had to help Elisabeth. He couldn't let her down.

She placed a pair of hip waders on the tractor. "Ready?"

Staring at the mucky water, he nodded. "I'll go in the water." Better him than her.

She drew her brows together. "Are you sure?"

No.

"Yes," he said, but she didn't look convinced. "You're better with the tractor."

"Not by much." She grinned. "You've really caught on."

Henry wished her compliment didn't mean so much to him. "Thanks. I had a good teacher."

Lately, everything Elisabeth said or did seemed important. Too important.

That was because she was his friend. But would a friend's opinion matter so much?

Knowing this wasn't the time to ponder that question, he snatched the hip waders and shoved his feet into them.

She handed him a screwdriver. "Use this to pry open the foot valve on the suction pipe. Make sure the valve is in the down position. Once the water drains, we can pull out the pipe. Any questions?"

About a million. He gripped the screwdriver. "None."

"Be careful."

He was more afraid of disappointing her than of the water.

With a nod, Henry waded to the center of the lake. He held the screwdriver in his teeth and lifted the pipe. It was heavier than he thought it would be. He struggled to get a good grip. It was wet and slimy and kept slipping. Using the screwdriver, he pried the valve open. Warm stinky water burst out, a poor man's version of Old Faithful, right onto his face.

It tasted worse than it smelled. He clamped his mouth closed and squeezed his eyes shut.

Make sure the valve is in the down position.

He'd forgotten. At least the water was draining. Goal accomplished. So what if he got blasted in the face? He'd gotten the job done. A satisfied feeling settled in the center of his chest. A feeling he'd only found working on the farm. He hoped he could take it with him when he left.

"Are you okay?" Elisabeth shouted.

He nodded and hoped she could see him.

She attached the pipe to the tractor, hopped into the seat, and started the engine. As the tractor moved forward on the wet ground, it heaved and slid toward the water.

It was going to roll.

Adrenaline surged. Henry took a step toward the shore but couldn't move farther because of the suction pipe in his hands. If he let go, it could seal the fate of the tractor and…

"Elisabeth."

Fear clawed at him. He'd never felt so useless, so helpless in his life. If she got hurt, it would be his fault. The drizzle turned into a downpour. Rain bombarded him and blurred the sight in front of him.

The engine revved, then almost stalled, but she didn't give up.

"You can do it," he yelled.

The water level rose, inch by inch. The continuous revving of the tractor engine prevented it from slipping again and rolling. Kept it from killing them.

A louder roar erupted when the tractor lurched forward

and pulled the pipe. Henry waded to shore with it, flashed her a thumbs-up, and returned to the irrigation equipment. They weren't finished yet. But the rest of the equipment came out easier.

As Elisabeth jumped out of the tractor, Henry climbed the muddy bank toward her. "You did it," he said.

A smile erupted on her face. "We did it."

Pride shot through him.

Elisabeth made her way to him. Her clothes were drenched and clinging to her.

Her gaze met his. Only falling rain and wet clothing separated them.

Henry took her into his arms, the way he'd been dreaming of doing for days, and kissed her. Long and hard. They were wet and muddy and sweaty. She'd never tasted so warm, so sweet.

He shouldn't be kissing her. Logically, that might be true, but only his mind told him to stop. His heart wanted to kiss her forever.

Forever?

No, for right now.

Elisabeth kissed him back with the same enthusiasm as she did everything else.

Holding her in his arms and kissing her was the best thing he'd done in a long while. Well, at least since he'd first kissed her. But this…this was better than that kiss. Everything about Elisabeth kept getting better. He wanted to know everything about her. He wanted to spend every minute with her.

He wanted to keep kissing her like this. He loved it.

Loved…

Henry tore his mouth away and stepped back. Elisabeth's flushed cheeks and swollen lips made him want to kiss her again and again. He stared into her eyes, eyes filled with desire and longing for him. She was perfect in every sense of the word.

The rain continued to fall on them. Drops ran down her face, resembling tears.

Reality came crashing back.

Henry wasn't looking for perfect. He wasn't looking for forever. He wasn't even looking for right now.

But if he were, he'd found it at the berry farm.

* * *

The following day, Elisabeth dragged herself out of the Suburban. Two shifts at the bistro had worn her out. She wanted to shower and go to bed, but that wasn't going to happen. Henry had picked up the kids from school and watched them for her. She appreciated his help, but she had no doubt that total chaos would await her inside.

Standing with her hand on the back doorknob, she tried to muster an extra ounce of energy. Her night was only beginning. She would have to clean up the kitchen, straighten up the living room, stick a load of laundry in, and…

Her shoulders slumped. She didn't want to think about everything she needed to do.

She opened the door and stepped inside. No food spills on the sparkling linoleum. No dishes on the gleaming countertops. Nothing out of place. The empty sink shone. Even the dish towels looked freshly washed.

This looked like her kitchen. No, this was cleaner than her kitchen.

She saw some clutter on the table. Thank goodness, or she would have thought she'd been transported to the twilight zone. A second glance showed her it wasn't a mess but decorations. A sign reading *Happy Unbirthday, Elisabeth* sat next to a very small pink-iced cake.

She placed her purse and jacket on a chair and walked into the living room. It was clean, too. All the toys had been picked up and books straightened. Sam sat on the couch. The television wasn't on, but music played from the old CD player in the corner.

He glanced up from the book on his lap and smiled. A smile? "Hi, Sis."

"Hey." She didn't know what else to say. "What are you reading?"

"Some stupid book."

"And you're reading it because…"

"Homework. I have to."

Except he didn't read. Not all his assignments, anyway. It was a constant complaint from his teachers that a boy as bright as Sam didn't always try.

"Oh, well, that's good," she said, trying not to show her surprise.

"Actually, it's not that bad." He twisted the book so she could read the title on the cover. *The Phantom Tollbooth*. "Henry said he read it when he was my age."

Henry. Of course.

"You had to work longer, so you missed the party," Sam said, changing the subject.

"I saw," she said. "Did you have fun?"

Sam shrugged. "It was okay. Abby and Caitlin had fun. We saved you a cake."

"Thank you."

"It was Henry's idea."

Elisabeth had figured that out. Everything good that happened around here turned out to be Henry's idea. She smiled.

"He's cool," Sam said. "I hope he sticks around."

Me, too. And that concerned her. They were all too attached to Henry. Elisabeth sighed. "Where are Henry and the girls?"

"Upstairs." Sam returned to his book. Homework, she corrected.

She heard a male voice coming from her room. She peeked in. Caitlin lay on the queen-size bed while Abby and Henry sat on the edge, reading.

"And the prince kissed the princess. The two moved to his castle on the hill and lived happily ever after. The end."

Henry closed the book and placed it on the nightstand. He tucked the blankets around Caitlin and kissed her forehead. "Good night, princess."

Caitlin giggled. "Good night, fairy daddy."

Holding her breath, Elisabeth waited for Henry to say something. He didn't. He merely ruffled Caitlin's curls.

Elisabeth exhaled slowly. Henry was such a natural with

children. No doubt about it, he was definite father material. Surely, he could feel it. No one could pretend the kind of affection he showed the kids.

Thanks to him, her brother and sisters had become happy children. The way they'd been before their parents' deaths. Henry had taught them, and her, how to laugh and live again. And Elisabeth knew then what she had been fighting all along—she was falling for him.

Who was she kidding? She'd fallen, headfirst, and was sinking deeper.

She loved Henry.

Elisabeth never thought she could feel this way about anyone, not after Toby. She hadn't wanted it to happen. She hadn't been looking for love but found it with Henry.

He made everything in her life seem brighter. Better. He showed her how much she had been missing out on by keeping herself closed off. He'd unlocked her heart and her soul.

So many changes. Good changes.

She didn't know what the future held, but she knew she didn't want to return to how things had been before Henry came to the farm. She couldn't, and neither could the kids.

He placed his arm around Abby. "Let's practice world capitals before your bedtime."

"I know them all."

"But I don't."

Elisabeth moved out of the doorway and waited for them in the hall. Waited and hoped. Perhaps he would want her and the kids. They deserved to be happy as much as anyone else.

Henry greeted her with a smile. "You're home."

Elisabeth nodded. "To a clean house. How did that happen?"

"We helped Henry," Abby said. "He didn't think you should come home to chores."

"Thanks."

"And we had a party like they had in *Alice in Wonderland*." Her eyes twinkled with excitement. "Did you see your unbirthday cake?"

"I did," Elisabeth said. "I like the pink icing."

"That was my idea. And Caitlin's." Abby grinned. "We used my Easy-Bake Oven to cook them."

"I had Sam standing by with a fire extinguisher just in case," Henry joked.

Elisabeth laughed.

"Oh, and Manny called," Abby said, heading into her bedroom.

"Manny said his mother is doing better," Henry said.

"That's great." Elisabeth was happy for Manny and his family but also confused at the mixed emotions churning inside her. She was relieved to finally hear the news she'd been waiting for and guilty for hoping he would stay away longer. "Did he say anything else?"

"Manny will be back next week."

Next week?

That was so soon. For her and the kids and Henry… What would he do? She started to ask but stopped herself. The answer was written in his eyes.

Henry hadn't said the words, but she had no doubt he would be leaving the farm. Just as she knew he would but had hoped with all her heart that he wouldn't.

Chapter Sixteen

I'm leaving.

A few days later, Henry sat at the kitchen table. Ten thirty in the morning and the kids were at school. He and Elisabeth had accomplished enough work on the evergreen blackberries to earn a coffee break. Talk about teamwork. Quite a change from his first day on the job. But thinking about the beginning reminded him of the end.

His official adventure would end in three days—a full month on the berry farm—but he wouldn't depart until Manny returned. Henry kept telling himself that was good enough. Elisabeth didn't need two farmhands. Not with winter approaching and money so tight. But the turmoil inside of Henry surprised him. He never thought he would feel this way when the day to say goodbye arrived.

That time was drawing near. He'd even emailed Frank,

using the free computer at the library, to keep him from showing up as originally scheduled.

But next week, he would be home.

Home.

The word no longer held the same appeal. His estate in Dunthorpe, a wealthy area just south of Portland, was large, with all the comforts anyone could imagine. Laurel Matthews and her interior design studio had seen to that during a massive remodel. But compared to this run-down farmhouse filled with kids, clutter, and animals, his elegant home and exciting life were suddenly, and strangely, unappealing.

But what had happened over the past month wasn't his life. No matter how well he'd adjusted to the work, he wasn't a farmer. And the Wheelers weren't his family.

He belonged to another world separate from the one he'd been living in during his adventure in Berry Patch. Though his real life seemed inconsequential and meaningless after one day on the farm.

Could Cynthia have been right?

Maybe he needed to rethink his over-the-top birthday parties and adventures. Maybe he needed to rethink a lot of things. Though not matchmaking. His friends still needed him to do that for them. Well, everyone except Elisabeth. He swirled the coffee in his mug.

But first, Henry needed to tell her he would be leaving. He'd tried on more than one occasion, but the words just wouldn't come. He'd stared into her blue eyes and wondered how it would feel to see them clouded with longing again like they were at the lake on that rainy day. He'd imagined waking up each morning gazing into them as their years together passed by. Those thoughts had rendered him speechless.

But those fantasies would never come true. He was playing a role. Henry the farmhand was simply a disguise—a ruse, so to speak—so far removed from his true identity it wasn't even funny. Sure, he'd been able to step out of his real world for a few weeks and see another side to life, a side he'd never imagined existed. Yes, being on the farm had been liberating, but his real life was in Portland. His real self was someone Elisabeth would never want to spend the rest of her life with.

He couldn't deny another truth, either. She hadn't asked him what his plans were. She hadn't said much about Manny returning. But sadness had descended over her, and that concerned Henry. They were tiptoeing around each other, walking on proverbial eggshells, trying to avoid the subject, but the tension would crack sooner rather than later. He downed the rest of his coffee.

The telephone rang, and Elisabeth answered it. "Hello." She paused. "Yes, this is her. What?" The horror in Elisabeth's voice made him look up. Her ghost-pale face had him rising from the table. She clutched the receiver until her knuckles went white. "W-which hospital?"

Hospital?

The million and one thoughts racing through Henry's mind were not good. He walked toward Elisabeth, never taking his eyes off her.

Her lower lip trembled, and she reached out for him.

Not one of the kids. It couldn't be one of the kids. He laced his fingers with hers and listened.

"Did she say—?"

She. Abby or Caitlin?

His stomach knotted, twisting and turning until he thought he would be physically ill.

"No, I understand." Tears welled in her eyes. "I'll be right there."

As she hung up the telephone, she took a deep breath. "Caitlin fell off the play structure at preschool. She hit her head. Or they think she did. She was unconscious. They've taken her to the hospital. I—I have to go."

"Let's go."

She grabbed her bag. "My keys?"

"I've got them." Henry grabbed her ring of keys off the counter. "I'll drive, and you navigate."

Her hands trembled. "Thank you."

She said the words, but she was simply going through the motions. Her eyes appeared unfocused, and the color hadn't returned to her face.

Henry couldn't imagine what was going through her head, not with what he was feeling. Driving kept him from losing it altogether. All he could think of was his tiny princess in a deep sleep. A kiss wouldn't wake her now. Henry hoped the doctors could.

The drive to the county hospital seemed to take forever. He tried to stay focused and get them there in one piece. This wasn't the time to make any mistakes. Not with so much at stake.

Still, a continuous stream of questions played in his head. Why wasn't someone watching Caitlin? How did she fall?

What sort of head injury? How long had she been unconscious?

Henry glanced over at Elisabeth, who sat with her hands clasped on her lap, the knuckles white. Her face was drawn tight, her entire body stiff.

He was worried sick. She must feel...

"How are you doing?" he asked.

Stupid question, but he didn't like that she was so quiet.

"I—I don't know." She blinked. "I just wish we were with her."

He removed his right hand from the steering wheel and held her hand, trying to offer a small amount of comfort and reassurance. "We'll be there soon."

"I'm glad you're driving. I don't think I could have..." Her voice cracked, and so did his heart. "Caitlin's never been afraid of heights. She loves to climb. She was so excited when she first went to the preschool and saw the play structure. I should have told her to stay off the top, but I never thought she'd fall."

"Caitlin would have climbed to the top, even if you told her not to. She's a kid."

"Probably, but..." Elisabeth choked on a sob. "What if Caitlin never wakes up? What if I lose her, too?"

Caitlin had asked him to be her daddy, and he'd said no. Regrets assailed him. What if he'd said yes?

He swallowed his anger to concentrate on Elisabeth. "Let's wait until we speak with the doctor before thinking the worst."

"You're right," Elisabeth said. "I know you're right."

He hoped so.

Henry parked the Suburban outside the emergency entrance of the county hospital. Elisabeth met him around the back of the SUV. Tears spiked her eyelashes, and he laced his fingers through hers.

She squeezed his hand. "I'm so glad you're here with me."

"Me, too." He expected her to release his hand, but she didn't. Together, they walked into the hospital with the same thought: Caitlin.

* * *

As Elisabeth headed to the information desk, she remembered making this same journey almost four years ago with a baby Caitlin in her arms and Sam and Abby at her sides. By the time they'd arrived, their parents were dead.

Tears stung Elisabeth's eyes, but she blinked them away. Thank goodness for Henry. He was her strength and her rock. She loved him. Pure and simple. He would be leaving, but he was there now. She clung to that.

"May I help you?" a smiling white-haired volunteer in a pink jacket asked.

"I'm looking for Caitlin Wheeler." Elisabeth tried to keep her voice steady. "She was brought in from the Berry Kids Preschool in Berry Patch."

"Oh, yes." The smile disappeared from the woman's face, and Elisabeth's pulse sped up. "Please take a seat. It'll be just a moment."

She didn't want to sit. That was what she'd done the last time she'd been there. "Do you mind if we stand?"

"Whichever you prefer." The woman rose.

A shiver of doom inched down Elisabeth's spine. She'd done the same thing waiting for news about her parents. "This isn't good."

"Hang in there." Henry squeezed her hand. "Caitlin will be okay."

Only one other person was in the waiting room. It was Mrs. Gavin, who operated the preschool. Eyes gleaming, she hurried over to them. "I'm so sorry, Elisabeth. Nothing like this has ever happened at our school."

Not trusting her voice, she nodded.

"I followed the ambulance. I didn't want Caitlin to be alone, but they wouldn't let me go into the exam area and won't give me any information since I'm not her guardian."

Elisabeth swallowed. "Thank you for being here with my sister. I appreciate it."

Mrs. Gavin's gaze bounced from Elisabeth to Henry. "Do you want me to stay?"

"No," she said quickly. "I'm sure you're needed at the preschool."

"We can let you know how Caitlin is doing," Henry added, much to Elisabeth's gratitude.

"Thank you, and we'll all be praying for Caitlin." With that, Mrs. Gavin headed toward the exit.

"Do you need something to drink?" Henry asked. "Anything?"

"No, thanks." Elisabeth stared at the double doors

leading to the exam rooms, willing them to open, but they remained closed. She swallowed a sigh.

A few minutes later, a young male doctor dressed in green scrubs walked up to them. "I'm Dr. Terrence. Are you Caitlin's parents?"

"I'm Elisabeth Wheeler, Caitlin's sister and guardian."

"Caitlin suffered a closed head trauma," he explained in a soothing tone. "There was a blow to her skull and a bruising of the brain—a concussion. She initially lost consciousness, regained it and complained of a bad headache when she woke up, and is now unconscious again. X-rays show a skull fracture, and that, with her presentation, suggests a possible epidural bleed."

Elisabeth wanted to shake him to upset his smooth delivery of such terrible news. This was her baby sister he was talking about.

"We aren't equipped to handle such traumas at this hospital," Dr. Terrence continued. "We need to get her to Portland Children's Hospital as soon as possible. Transportation is being arranged, and a team of specialists, including a neurosurgeon, will be waiting."

"Whatever you need to do, do it." Her voice sounded shrill. She cleared her throat. "I just want her to get better."

Henry tightened his fingers around hers. She was so thankful he was with her. She couldn't imagine going through this alone.

"We're doing everything we can," Dr. Terrence said. "It's imperative we move quickly. Do you have insurance?"

"Forget about the cost," Henry interrupted. "What's important is getting Caitlin the best care available. Right, Elisabeth?"

All she could manage was a nod. But Henry was right. If it took selling the farm, selling everything to pay for the medical care, so be it. All that mattered was Caitlin.

"You can see her while we make final preparations," Dr. Terrence said.

Elisabeth and Henry followed the doctor through a set of double doors. In the center of the emergency department, doctors and nurses milled around a busy hub containing computers, monitors, and phones. Around the perimeter of the central area were glass-enclosed examining areas. The doctor opened a sliding glass door to one of the rooms.

Caitlin lay on a gurney, a bandage on the side of her head. Machines beeped and blinked.

No, this couldn't be happening. Not to Caitlin. Not to her baby.

Anguish tore into Elisabeth, weakened her knees, and she collapsed against Henry. He embraced her, sharing his strength and comfort. She needed both from him. And so much more.

"She's so pale. So little." Elisabeth reached out and touched Caitlin's ashen skin. "She feels cold. Do you think she needs another blanket?"

Henry pulled up a chair for Elisabeth to sit on. "I'll find a nurse."

She sat but didn't know what else to do. She reached for her sister's small hand.

"It's going to be okay, sweetie." An IV ran into Caitlin's other arm. A lump formed in Elisabeth's throat, but if she cried, it would be all over with. "We're going to a hospital in Portland."

No response. Fear shuddered through Elisabeth. It was all she could do not to fall into a heap on the gray tile floor. But she couldn't. She had to be strong for Caitlin.

"Portland is where Henry used to live," Elisabeth said. "The hospital is especially for kids."

She glanced at the nurses' station in the center of the emergency department. Henry spoke to a group of people. A woman dressed in a suit handed a phone to Henry, and he looked serious. A little too serious.

Elisabeth looked away. She couldn't deal with any more bad news right now.

"Henry's here." She touched Caitlin's rose-petal-smooth cheek. "He's making sure the doctors take good care of you. And he's taking good care of me, too."

Elisabeth kissed Caitlin's hand. She was afraid to touch anything else.

"You're going to get better." The machines beeped and blinked. All good signs, she assumed. "Don't worry. It'll be okay. You'll be fine."

She had to be. Because if not, Elisabeth didn't know what she would do.

* * *

As Henry watched Elisabeth in the exam room, her misery and pain pressed down on him like a steel beam. It wasn't fair.

She didn't deserve this. And Caitlin…

She should be smiling and giggling and jumping around. A hospital bed was no place for such a vibrant little girl.

He had more money than he knew what to do with, yet he couldn't make her better. He couldn't buy his way out of this situation. It was exactly how he felt when Wes was diagnosed with cancer. That same helpless, worthless feeling.

Sure, Caitlin would have the top specialists and the best care available, and it wouldn't cost the Wheelers anything. Henry had seen to that. If only he could do more…

Elisabeth's gaze locked with his. The weight of the world once again rested on her tired shoulders, and he couldn't do anything to make her feel better. It took every ounce of his strength to smile, but he did.

For her sake.

Dr. Terrence returned with a nurse. "Caitlin's blood pressure is increasing. This could mean the pressure in her brain is also increasing. She needs to go now." He emphasized the last word. "A Life Flight helicopter is on its way. Everything will be ready for Caitlin when she arrives at the hospital."

Elisabeth's lower lip quivered. Henry placed his arm around her and led her outside.

Standing there, she wrapped her arms around her chest. "I'm scared."

"Me, too." Henry pulled her close. "Two of my closest friends will be waiting for you at the hospital. Brett and Laurel Matthews will keep you company until I arrive."

Elisabeth stepped away from him. "You aren't going with me?"

Her disappointment stabbed at him. "There isn't room on the Life Flight helicopter for us. Another helicopter will follow that one, but they only have space for one passenger."

"They do that?"

"In certain instances." He didn't want to tell the truth: that he'd made the arrangements for the second helicopter so Elisabeth wouldn't have to be away from Caitlin that long. "I'll pick up Sam and Abby from school. They need to hear what happened from one of us, not a schoolteacher or administrator, and I'll drive them to the hospital in Portland."

Elisabeth nodded. "And I need someone to watch the farm—"

"I called Gabe. He and his father are on it."

More than gratitude shone in her eyes, and he felt like he'd been run over by the Deere. The edges of her mouth curved slightly. "Thank you."

Don't thank me, he wanted to yell. This was driving him crazy. The feeling of helplessness overwhelmed him, and he hated it. He hated feeling so useless. He hated caring the way he did. About Caitlin and Sam and Abby. But most especially about Elisabeth.

She caressed his cheek. "I don't know what I'd do without you."

He felt the same way, but he couldn't bring himself to say the words. No matter how he felt about Elisabeth and the rest of the Wheelers, she didn't need him blurting out his feelings, diverting attention from the sister she loved. The sister she had gladly taken responsibility for, the way he'd never taken responsibility for anything or anyone in his life.

More people entered Caitlin's room. The doctor barked

orders. Nurses hurried. Things happened so fast. Suddenly, Caitlin was wheeled out of the room on the gurney.

"Let's go," Dr. Terrence said, his voice full of urgency.

Henry walked with them until he was told he could go no farther. He wanted to go with them. He wanted to be there for them. But he also wanted to be there for Sam and Abby, who would need someone with them.

"Have a safe flight." Henry didn't know what else to say. "I'll be at the hospital as soon as I can."

That was all he could promise her. Once again, it wasn't enough.

As Elisabeth, the doctors, and the nurses disappeared behind a pair of elevator doors, a deep pain gnawed at Henry. He waited what he thought was long enough that the helicopters must have lifted off and were on their way to Portland. With his heart in his throat, he returned to the hospital lobby, found a phone, and dialed out.

"I wondered when I would be hearing from you," Cynthia said, sounding smug and satisfied. "How's your adventure going down on the farm?"

Only two words needed to be said, but he was having a difficult time saying them. He didn't understand why. He'd made the right choice. The right choice for Caitlin. The right choice for Elisabeth. The right choice for him.

The only choice.

Henry knew that in his heart, but his life would never be the same. Maybe that was why saying the words were so hard. He inhaled deeply and exhaled slowly.

"Henry?" Cynthia asked.

It was now or never. "You win."

Chapter Seventeen

The Portland Children's Hospital was newer than the county hospital. That explained why everything there was fresh and bright to appeal to young patients. The facility impressed Elisabeth, but she was lost.

Alice had a better chance of finding her way back through the looking glass than Elisabeth had in locating the waiting room. She must have made a wrong turn when she walked out of the restroom. Or several. Worst of all, she couldn't find a floor plan or a map anywhere. Even the signs seemed to lead her astray.

I'm walking around in circles.

Of course, she'd felt the same way ever since the neurosurgeon had spoken to her after examining Caitlin. His words kept swirling through Elisabeth's head. An acute bleed was putting pressure on Caitlin's brain. She needed immediate surgery. Something about a pressure probe being inserted into her skull. Relieving pressure by evacuating the hematoma. It was all very confusing and frightening. The doctor had also talked about the risks—permanent nerve damage, permanent brain damage, death—and alternatives to surgery—none.

Elisabeth shivered. That seemed like hours ago, but maybe she'd just lost track of time. A part of her wished this was nothing more than a nightmare, but the pain was too real for her to be dreaming.

Where was Henry?

She wished he would arrive and glanced around as if he would magically appear. Funny, but she wouldn't put that past him, given everything else he'd done for her.

His friends had been waiting for her as he'd promised. They'd met her just inside the hospital from the helicopter pad as if they'd been tracking the flight plan. Laurel, an interior designer and mother of Henry's goddaughter, greeted Elisabeth with a hug and handed her a bottle of water to drink. Her husband, Brett, a financial adviser who seemed like an all-around nice guy, was also Henry's best friend. Brett had told her that he would deal with admission details and only asked her for help if he couldn't answer a question. Elisabeth was so appreciative of that since they were strangers to her. However, she realized Brett had been one of the references Cynthia had given for Henry, so this was Elisabeth's second time speaking with him.

She wanted to get back to Laurel and Brett and wait for an update from the doctor.

As she wandered around the floor, Elisabeth realized nothing looked familiar. Was this still the same wing?

Trying to make her way back to the waiting room, Elisabeth passed a dozen pink roses in a crystal vase and a stuffed pony sitting on the top shelf of a cart. Caitlin would love the stuffed animal. If only she were here to see it...

Emotion clogged Elisabeth's throat. Her sister had to be okay. She just had to be.

Standing at an intersection of three hallways, Elisabeth's vision blurred. She rubbed her eyes, deciding to go straight. The left and right hallways hadn't led her to the waiting area where she'd left Laurel and Brett. That much she knew.

Elisabeth needed to get back. She needed news about Caitlin's status. She needed Henry.

What was keeping him?

She couldn't wait to see Henry. He would help her ignore the antiseptic smell in the air. He would help her see things weren't as horrible as they seemed. He would help her feel better.

Her work boots against the sanitary tile floor echoed through the hallway. She walked past the same bank of elevators. Again.

Her shoulders slumped, and tears welled once again. She blinked, not wanting to break down out in the open.

Elisabeth took a breath and another. All she needed was to be pointed in the right direction. If she waited in one spot, maybe someone would come by who could show her the way.

As she leaned against the wall, she noticed a bronze plaque engraved with a dedication hanging opposite her.

The C. & L. Davenport Wing of Portland Children's Hospital was donated by Henry Davenport in memory of his parents, Charles and Lillian Davenport.

Elisabeth squinted to reread the words.

Henry…Davenport? *Her* Henry Davenport?

Except Henry had nothing. Yet…hadn't Cynthia said he'd lost everything? Maybe before his misfortune, Henry had donated a whole hospital wing?

Elisabeth bit her lip, confused. No, that wasn't possible. Yet if it were him…

To go from all that to nothing.

Pride in Henry overflowed. After losing everything, he hadn't given up. He'd taken the job at the berry farm and kept going. Her respect for him grew tenfold. As did her love. She touched Henry's name on the plaque.

The elevators opened, and a nurse dressed in blue scrubs exited.

Elisabeth jerked her hand away from the engraving. "Excuse me, do you know how to get to the neurosurgery waiting room?"

The nurse nodded and pointed. "Down this hall and make the first left and another right."

"Thanks." Elisabeth glanced back at the plaque. She wanted to know the truth but didn't want to embarrass Henry by asking Brett and Laurel.

"Do you know him?" Elisabeth asked impulsively, half expecting to be told Henry Davenport was a carbon copy of Mr. Jackson, a balding, rotund businessman in his sixties. "Henry Davenport."

"Yes, he's very generous, especially when it comes to children. He drops off presents for the patients here," the nurse explained. "The kids call him their fairy godfather."

Caitlin had called him "fairy daddy." Elisabeth thought about everything Henry had done for them. He'd been like a real-life fairy godfather to all of them this past month.

Her heart lurched. A coincidence. It had to be a coincidence, right?

"That's thoughtful of him," Elisabeth said weakly.

The nurse nodded. "Did you know he donated money for a new neonatal intensive care unit? They break ground next month."

That didn't make any sense. Not if it was her Henry. Elisabeth's spirits brightened. "Really?"

"Surprising, I know." The nurse grinned. "You'd never think someone like him would care so much about children. I mean, he's a rich playboy who dates famous models and actresses and pretty much anything with a decent pair of legs."

A rich playboy?

It couldn't be. He couldn't be. Yet…

Elisabeth struggled to breathe. "I had no idea."

"You must not pay attention to the society page, then, honey. He's always in there and never with the same date." The nurse checked her pager. "I have to go."

So did Elisabeth. She needed to ask Brett and Laurel about Henry. They were nice. They would explain what was going on.

She hurried down the hall, following the nurse's directions to the waiting room. She sighed in relief when she saw the maroon and forest-green modular furniture offering plenty of seating choices. A muted TV was tuned to a financial channel. The sedate and calming wall color made the room feel cozier and less institutional.

Laurel straightened the skirt of her gray dress. Her blue eyes clouded with concern. "We were getting worried."

Elisabeth was worried, too. "I got lost." In more ways than one. "Any word?"

"No." Brett stood. He was as handsome as his wife was beautiful. His dark brown hair curled at the ends, and his chocolate-brown eyes softened every time he looked at Laurel. "Would you like a cup of coffee or a soda?"

"No, thanks." Elisabeth wiped her sweaty palms on her faded and torn blue jeans. "But I would like to talk to you about Henry."

"What do you want to know?" Brett asked.

Elisabeth tasted blood and stopped biting the inside of her cheek. She had to be wrong, simply letting her imagination run wild. "If Henry lost all his money and is homeless, how can he afford to build a new neonatal intensive care unit for this hospital?"

The troubled glance shared by Laurel and Brett told Elisabeth she wouldn't like the answer.

"You should probably sit down," Laurel said.

Elisabeth sat, took a deep breath, and prepared herself. For what, she didn't know. But from the looks of things, it wouldn't be good.

Laurel sat next to her. "Henry means the world to Brett and me. He's a generous, caring man who loves to have a good time."

"*Fun* is Henry's middle name," Brett added.

"But he's also a bit…eccentric. A cross between Cupid and a fairy godfather," Laurel explained. "Henry enjoys throwing himself elaborate birthday parties and creating wild adventures to send two friends on so he can play matchmaker. That's how Brett and I met. Cynthia met Cade that way in April."

April wasn't *that* long ago, which confused Elisabeth even more. "How could Henry afford to do that if he lost everything? I don't understand."

"Henry didn't lose all his money." Brett sat on the other side of her. "He hasn't lost any."

Her apprehension grew. "He has…money?"

"Henry is extremely…well off," Brett said.

A rich playboy… Her mind reeled.

"Cynthia thought it was time to teach Henry a lesson because he thinks he knows what's best for his friends. Henry also enjoys playing matchmaker with his friends outside of his birthday too. Anyway, she decided to give him a taste of his own medicine, but she also wanted to show him that most people aren't in his position and can't throw money around to make things better." The look in Laurel's eyes softened. Or was that pity? "Cynthia sent Henry on his own adventure to your berry farm."

Elisabeth felt as if her breath had been cut off and her chest would burst. But she held herself together. She needed to know more. "Please tell me everything."

Brett explained about being the son of the Davenports' housekeeper and growing up with Henry, and about Wes Lockhart, introducing Henry to his friends, who later became known as the Billionaires of Silicon Forest, and how Henry had played matchmaker with all six of them. Laurel told her how Henry was a well-known philanthropist, who'd donated billions of dollars, and how he had two godchildren because of his matchmaking efforts and wanted more so he could spoil them and make them his heirs since he didn't plan on marrying or having a family of his own.

Elisabeth's hands tightened so much her knuckles turned white. She didn't speak. She couldn't. Not when she sat stunned and numbed by the truth.

Henry wasn't poor and homeless. He was a billionaire who loved having fun. He wasn't interested in the farm or having a family or her. He'd been playing games with Elisabeth from the start.

Brett and all the other references had all been a part of Cynthia's plan. Cynthia had gotten the twenty-five thousand dollars from her boss, Wes Lockhart. They had all…lied to Elisabeth, including Henry.

Especially Henry.

"I understand now," Elisabeth forced through tight lips. She had to get out of here. Now.

Another worried glance passed between Brett and his wife. Brett's eyes narrowed. "Are you okay?"

"I need to use the restroom again." Elisabeth picked up her purse and stood. "Excuse me, please."

Laurel rose. "Want some company?"

"No…thanks. I know my way now and won't get lost this time." A faint hysteria laced the words. As Elisabeth left the waiting room, she reversed the directions and found the restroom quickly, but with each step, she struggled for control.

She refused to cry. She'd wasted too many tears on Toby. She wouldn't do the same with Henry.

When she got inside, Elisabeth splashed water on her face. She didn't know what else to do.

Henry had lied to her.

She ached with a pain so ragged, so deep, she feared the hurt would never go away.

Everything had been a lie.

The laughter, the smiles, the kisses. His time on the farm had been nothing more than a rich man's adventure. A joke. A bet. Payback for him putting his friends at the mercy of his whims.

Toby might have broken her heart, but Henry had shattered it beyond repair. That wasn't even the worst part. This time, the kids were involved. Sam, Abby, and Caitlin had fallen in love with Henry too. He'd brought smiles to their faces, laughter to their hearts, joy to their lives. He'd changed them; he'd changed everything. The kids would be devastated.

What would Elisabeth tell them?

She dried her face.

Tell them the truth.

That Henry was only planning to work at the farm temporarily, and his time was up. The kids didn't need to know any more than that. She could save them from finding out he'd lied to them.

Besides, all of them had known Henry would leave when Manny returned. Though Elisabeth hadn't understood why if he had no job or home to go to. She'd hoped they could change his mind. That *she* would change his mind.

She'd been a fool. Such a fool.

Of course he wouldn't stay.

The nurse's words tortured Elisabeth. *He's a rich playboy who dates famous models and actresses.*

Not poor, boring farm girls from Berry Patch.

All her energy, all her strength drained. She sagged against a tiled wall.

No. She couldn't give up. Elisabeth straightened. She wouldn't let Henry do that to her. His lies hurt, but she would recover. And so would the kids after he left. They had no other choice.

She opened her purse, found her cell phone, and opened her payment app. Elisabeth had never transferred Cynthia's money to her bank account. A part of her had been afraid to.

Elisabeth stared at all the zeros. She needed the twenty-five thousand dollars, especially with Caitlin's head injury, but it had been given to her under false pretenses. So had the help. There was only one thing she could do—return the money.

With a trembling hand, she sent the money back to Cynthia, who could repay her boss.

Henry's adventure was over.

He could stop lying and start laughing. About his time spent on the struggling farm. About three orphaned kids. About her.

But Elisabeth had a sinking feeling it would be a long time before she or any of the kids would feel like laughing again.

Chapter Eighteen

Rain pelted the windshield, and Henry struggled to see the highway. Luckily, there wasn't much traffic on I-5, but once they hit Wilsonville…

He fiddled with the knobs on the radio, searching for a traffic report, but heard only static. He turned it off. The two kids sitting in the middle row of the Suburban were quiet. "You guys okay?"

"Is Caitlin dead?" Sam asked.

Henry felt as if his heart had been ripped out of his chest. Suddenly, quiet didn't seem so bad. "She's at the hospital."

"My parents were at the hospital, but they were dead by the time we got there," Abby said. "Caitlin could be dead."

Nausea swept over Henry. He needed to be there with Elisabeth.

"Caitlin's dead, isn't she?" Sam asked. "You're just not telling us."

Henry gripped the steering wheel. "Your sister was stable when I last saw her."

"But that was hours ago," Abby said. "Anything could have happened since then, and we wouldn't know. You don't have a cell phone."

Sometimes Abby was too smart for her own good. He grimaced. "No worst-case-scenario thinking. The doctors are doing everything they can."

Silence swallowed the car. Or as much silence as one could have in the middle of a rainstorm on a major interstate.

"Was Elisabeth crying when you left her?" Abby asked.

Henry weighed his options. He didn't want to upset the kids, nor did he want to lie. "She was upset."

"She never cries," Abby announced.

Henry had seen Elisabeth cry. The night he'd found her in the living room air-harping. "Never?"

"Not since Toby left," Sam answered.

"Toby?" Henry asked.

"He was going to marry Elisabeth," Abby explained.

"He was a jerk," Sam said. "He dumped her."

That must be the guy she'd mentioned to him. Any man who would leave Elisabeth was definitely a jerk. The thought made Henry squirm.

"Sometimes adults have reasons for what they do, even if it appears bad at the time," he said carefully, hoping they all, especially Elisabeth, would understand his actions this past month. "Reasons maybe they can't explain or that don't make sense to kids."

"Oh, Toby had reasons," Sam said. "He didn't want us."

Henry glanced in the rearview mirror. "Didn't want…?"

"Me, Abby, and Caitlin. And Elisabeth wouldn't leave us," Sam admitted. "She said we were a package deal and gave Toby his ring back. Then she cried for a week."

"I don't remember an entire week of crying," Abby said.

Sam gave her a lofty look. "You were too little then."

Henry barely heard their bickering. Guilt deafened him. Swamped him. He'd originally thought the same thing about not wanting to settle down and have kids. But that had changed. He'd changed.

The Wheelers were a package deal. One he wanted.

Up till now, his life had been meaningless. His parties and adventures were fun, but nothing compared to the life he'd found on the farm.

With Elisabeth.

He'd tried to avoid responsibility. He'd tried to hang on to control. He'd tried not to let any of the Wheelers get close.

He'd failed on every front.

"Are you going to leave, too?" Sam probed.

Henry had intended to.

But now…

The thought of losing Caitlin terrified him. He didn't pray—didn't know the right way to pray—but he still prayed she would be okay. But if she recovered and he left, wouldn't he lose her just the same? Lose her and Abby and Sam.

Lose Elisabeth.

What a jerk.

The Wheelers had welcomed him into their home, into their lives, and into their hearts. They loved him for him. Not his name. Not his wallet. It was what he'd needed all along, but he hadn't known it until now. Henry might not have started out as a family man, but that was what he'd become, and he wanted to remain one.

"I don't want to leave."

It was the truth. He could admit it to this boy when he'd barely acknowledged the truth to himself. Henry wanted to be a husband, a father, and a farmer. The best farmer Berry Patch had ever known. He wanted it all—love, marriage, and a happily ever after. Not only for himself but also for all the Wheelers. Especially Elisabeth.

Henry still had a lot to learn, but he was ready. He wanted the opportunity to try to be the man Elisabeth deserved in her life.

Would she be willing to give him the chance?

* * *

Henry ushered Abby out of the elevator on the neurosurgery floor at the Children's Hospital, but Sam hung back. "Let's go."

He stared at the floor. "Are you sure this is the right way?"

Of course. Henry had paid for this wing to be built. He'd seen the blueprints before the foundation had been poured. He'd visited every floor both during construction and after. But Sam didn't know that, and now wasn't the time to tell him.

Henry knew Sam was worried. He didn't blame the kid, but Elisabeth needed them to get there. Traffic had made the drive longer than it should've been. "Yes, and we need to get going. Elisabeth has been waiting for you two to arrive."

Abby held his hand. "And you, too."

He hoped so. The three of them walked to the waiting room, which was filled with his friends. He'd expected Brett and Laurel to be there but not Wes, Paige, Blaise, Hadley, Dash, Cynthia, and even his chauffeur, Frank. "What are you all doing here?"

"Group chat," Dash said. "The others will be here soon."

Cynthia approached him, but she wasn't gloating as he expected. If anything, she appeared worried. She handed Henry his phone. "Cade's been out of town, but he's catching a flight back tonight. Brynn's training in Vermont, but Ryland will be here tomorrow."

"Thanks." Henry appreciated his friends—all people he'd played matchmaker with—for wanting to be there with him, but someone was missing. He kept looking around. "Where's Elisabeth?"

"With Caitlin."

Henry released the breath he'd been holding. He needed to find Elisabeth and see Caitlin, but then he remembered the kids. "Abby and Sam, meet my friends."

"More like his family," Wes said, and everyone nodded.

Paige came up to him and the kids. She wore her physician's jacket. "Caitlin is recovering after her surgery."

"She's not dead?" Sam asked.

The waiting room went silent.

Paige touched Sam's shoulder. "Caitlin is still

unconscious. Her medical team is watching your sister to make sure the pressure in her brain goes down."

Abby clung to Henry's hand, but she stared in awe of Paige. "Are you my sister's doctor?"

Paige smiled at her. "No, but I'm a doctor, an oncologist, and I was with your sister Elisabeth when she spoke to Caitlin's neurosurgeon."

Relief surged through Henry. He was so grateful Paige, who'd treated Wes when he'd had cancer, had been with Elisabeth. "Thank you."

"Caitlin's medical team is taking good care of her," Paige said. "We can ask if you can see her after Elisabeth comes out."

Abby nodded.

Sam scrubbed at his eyes. "Please."

Dash came up to the kids with a large shopping bag. He towered over them at six-three but lowered himself to their level and smiled. "I'm Dash. My wife, Iris, had to stay home with our son, but she sent homemade brownies for you on the table over there, and I picked up something for you guys." Dash pulled two new Nintendo Switch boxes from the bag. "There's one for each of you. I have another one for Caitlin."

The kids stared in disbelief. Their mouths each formed a perfect *O*.

Leave it to Dash. The guy had come a long way from the clueless, selfish genius who didn't know how to handle social situations well. He'd made up for all his mistakes to Iris and then some.

Henry smiled. "Thanks, Master Dashiell."

"Least I could do," Dash said to Henry. "Fallon has kids around Abby's age, so that helped. And who doesn't like video games?"

Fallon was Dash's assistant and Blaise's sister-in-law. Henry had fun watching "Uncle Blaise" in action with his niece and nephew. He looked at the kids. "I'm sure these two will enjoy them."

Sam clutched the game as if it were a priceless artifact. "It's brand new."

"Not for long." Dash grinned. "Go on and open it."

Both kids looked at Henry as if asking for permission. They were such good kids. Elisabeth would be proud. "It's okay. Dash is a good friend."

"But these are really expensive." Abby tried to whisper, but everyone could hear her. "If we break it, we won't be able to afford to replace it."

No one said a word. Wes held back a smile. He'd grown up wealthy like Henry. Dash hadn't nor had Blaise, but both were billionaires now.

"It's okay, Abby," Henry said to her in a low voice. "Dash bought this as a gift for you and Sam, so don't worry about replacing it."

She didn't appear convinced, so he would try again. "Dash has a good job, so you don't have to worry about what it cost him, okay?"

The kids still didn't move. Henry was struck by how these kids probably knew more about budgeting and saving money than he ever would. He looked at Dash for help, who brushed his hand through his hair.

"I have an idea." Dash pointed at an empty couch on the far side of the waiting room. "I see an outlet over there. How about we sit and get these set up for you while Henry checks in on your sisters?"

The kids glanced at Henry again, and he nodded. Finally, the kids relaxed, and Henry could, too. As Abby and Sam followed Dash, Henry watched them go.

Frank came up to him. "Don't worry about the kids. I'll guard them with my life."

With that, Frank headed over to Abby and Sam and offered to help Dash set up their controllers. Frank was one of the best bodyguards in the business, and Dash would make sure the kids were safe. Henry trusted both men but still kept glancing Abby and Sam's way. He needed to know they were okay.

"So…" Cynthia bit her lip. "Elisabeth returned the money."

"What money?" Henry asked, confused.

"The twenty-five thousand dollars I gave her."

He did a double take. "What are you talking about?"

"The cost of the adventure." Cynthia blew out a breath. "I offered Elisabeth money I got from Wes if she hired you. I also told her I'd cover your salary, which I still want to do, even though she doesn't want to accept it."

The money would make such a difference to the farm. "Why would she return it?"

Brett came up. "Elisabeth saw the donation plaque with your and your parents' names on it. She knows everything, including your adventures. We could tell she wasn't happy with what she heard, but she never said a word. She was polite to everyone who showed up, even those who were Cynthia's references, and lied to her about your *situation*. Elisabeth seems to be a strong woman, but she's very hurt."

"She is strong." The kids seemed too busy to notice what anyone else was doing. Both laughed at something Dash said. That was good. Henry sighed. He should've known this would happen, but he thought everything would be okay. The way things usually turned out for him. "I'm sure the truth devastated her, but it was a risk I had to take."

This hospital was the best place for Caitlin, and the middle of a life-threatening medical emergency hadn't been the time for him to come clean to Elisabeth. Not that he'd planned on doing that.

Henry rubbed his face.

Cynthia's eyes gleamed. "I'm so sorry how things turned out. This was supposed to teach you a lesson."

Henry half laughed. "Oh, it did."

"I also wanted you to have fun."

"That's what I always say." Hearing Cynthia repeat the words drove home how his friends must have felt, even if they were living happily ever after now. "But sometimes the fun can get carried away."

Brett's forehead creased. "That doesn't sound like the Henry Davenport I know. What happened while you were in Berry Patch?"

Henry stared at Abby and Sam, who showed Frank their game controllers. "I found more family."

Chapter Nineteen

In the neurosurgical ICU, Elisabeth sat next to Caitlin's bed. Her sister had yet to regain consciousness after the surgery and looked so tiny and vulnerable under the blanket. She remembered what the neurosurgeon had told her.

Bleeding controlled. Minimal edema. No obvious death of brain matter.

The doctor had been pleased with the surgery's outcome, and that kept Elisabeth from losing all hope, especially with Dr. Regis-Lockhart explaining everything in understandable terms. Elisabeth was grateful to have the other doctor with her, but seeing her baby sister like this was so hard.

Bandages covered Caitlin's entire head. Tubes and wires were attached to her body, including a catheter going into her skull. All the beeps and noises from the machines with too many displays and graphs and buttons scared Elisabeth, but something else terrified her. The surgery, medical care, and doctors would be expensive. So, so expensive. Selling the farm might not even be able to cover the bills, and where would that leave them? Bankrupt?

Stop.

Guilt coated her throat. She shouldn't worry about money while Caitlin lay in that bed, fighting for her life. They would have plenty of time to figure out the finances.

Still, Elisabeth felt as if she hung by a thread. She was brokenhearted and hurting because of Caitlin and Henry.

Forget about Henry. Concentrate on Caitlin. She was so small and fragile and pale. She was the one who needed Elisabeth.

"You're my little girl. I love you so much. You must get better. I don't think I could take it if one more person I love went away." Elisabeth rested her head on the bed. The rhythm of the machines was almost hypnotic but far from soothing. "Wake up, Caitlin. Please wake up."

Elisabeth sensed a presence behind her. One of the nurses who sat in the central core area where they monitored and watched the patients?

Hands touched her shoulders, and she knew.

Henry.

She inhaled sharply. Every muscle tensed. Relief mixed with frustration, and she wavered. But she knew after discovering the truth, the only thing she could do was erect a wall between them to keep from being hurt more.

"Sam and Abby are in the waiting room with my friends," Henry began. "The report from the doctor sounds promising."

Elisabeth focused on the icy fear twisting in her stomach and the panic rioting inside her. "Caitlin's still not awake."

"Give her time."

Elisabeth was furious at her vulnerability to Henry. She hated that she needed his reassurance. She shouldn't want or need anything from him. "What if time is running out?"

The question stabbed at her heart. The prognosis was good, but she was still so frightened, so worried. And to have Henry show up… She trembled.

Henry squeezed Elisabeth's shoulders. "It won't."

Not for Caitlin, Elisabeth prayed. But for herself and Henry…

She wanted to hurt him, but she wanted to make him want her at the same time. "I know who you are." Her voice sounded steadier than she felt. "When were you going to tell me the truth?"

He hesitated.

Loneliness and confusion, frustration and anger welded together. But she had her pride. He couldn't take that from her. "I deserved the truth. Then and now."

She felt the breath he drew.

"The truth," he agreed. "I didn't plan to tell you."

She didn't think it was possible to feel any more pain. She'd been wrong.

"Ever?" She held her breath.

Again, that slight hesitation. "No."

Her heart died within her. She'd always known. But to hear him say it…

She didn't fall into a heap. She didn't slump in her chair.

Instead, her blood boiled. Her cheeks grew hot with humiliation. She pinned him with her eyes. "You were just going to leave."

"Elisabeth…"

She pressed her lips together. "The truth."

"Okay. I was planning to leave. But—"

"I don't want to hear any of your excuses." She spat out the words. "Just go back to your world and leave us alone."

"You are my world." He touched her hand, and she jerked away. "You, Sam, Abby, Caitlin, Ruff, Ritz, even that damn rooster who *cock-a-doodle-doos* all day long."

Some part of her had longed to hear those words and wanted to believe him. But she couldn't. This wasn't Henry, the down-on-his-luck farmhand, talking. This was Henry, the billionaire. The liar. "I don't believe you."

"It's the truth," he mumbled.

The pain in her voice made her want to reach out to him. She couldn't. "But you're rich and have a whole other life. Without us."

Without me.

Saying the words made them more real. Bitterness filled her, and anguish squeezed her heart. Henry might think he wanted them at first, but he would leave.

A rich playboy… Never with the same date.

"I know all about your 'adventure.'" She struggled to hold on to her composure and her pride. "I returned Cynthia's twenty-five thousand dollars."

His eyes darkened. "That's a lot of money."

"Not to you." Elisabeth knew she was acting like a bratty kid, but she didn't care. She couldn't care. Not about him.

"Elisabeth—"

"No matter what your intentions, I appreciate you working on the farm." She straightened. "If you leave me your address, I'll mail your final paycheck."

"I don't need the check. I need you."

She shrugged, ignoring how the desperation in his voice clawed at her. She didn't know what to do. Conflicting emotions were turning her inside out. She couldn't take it. Not now. Probably not ever. "It's better this way. You must have places to go, money to spend, women to woo."

His eyebrows drew together. "Woo?"

"Or whatever it is you do with them. You've been on a boring berry farm for a month. I'm sure you need to make up for lost time."

Tears stung her eyes. She focused on Caitlin so he wouldn't see. This was for the best. If Henry remained in her life, he would never be happy. He would leave her. Leave the kids, too. Elisabeth preferred he did it now.

"What are you saying?" he asked.

"Goodbye, Henry."

As she stared at one of the monitors, she waited. Beeping, blips, breathing. Then she heard footsteps moving away from her. She listened until they were gone.

The strength she'd been clinging to vanished, leaving her lost and dejected and with nothing.

Despite the lies, despite everything, a part of her had still hoped Henry would be different. That he wasn't like the others who went away or died and left her alone.

An acute sense of loss overcame her. Elisabeth clenched

her hands into fists. A lump burned in her throat as hot as a glowing charcoal briquette, but she would not cry. The kids, especially Caitlin, needed Elisabeth to be strong now. She had the rest of her life to fall apart.

The machines kept making noises, and she focused on those.

Footsteps sounded again. Only this time, they were coming toward her. Closer and closer. Her breath caught in her throat.

It must be a nurse or doctor. Still, she clutched the bed rail.

"I won't let you do this," Henry said in a firm tone. "I heard what you said to Caitlin about another person you loved going away. I'm not like the others. I won't leave you. And I won't let you push me away."

Elisabeth had to push. She had no choice but to be the one to send him away. Because if he was the one to leave her, she didn't think she would survive. And she had to endure. For Sam and Abby and—Elisabeth stared at the hospital bed—Caitlin.

He stopped right behind her. "I've never had to fight for anything in my life, but I'll fight for you, Elisabeth with an *S*. And I won't lose."

"Don't do this." She choked on the words, battling the desperation threatening to overwhelm her. Her knuckles blanched on the bed rail. "Stop saying things you don't mean."

Henry gently pried her hands off it and turned her so she faced him. A million and one thoughts ran through Elisabeth's head. "Why are you doing this?"

"I'm not going away." His eyes implored her with a need that had her back hitting the bed. "I need you and the kids."

Such simple words. She didn't want to believe him. She shouldn't, yet he was somehow breaking through her fragile control. She trembled and tried to fight it, fight him. She gritted her teeth. "You lied."

He bowed his head. "I let you down."

"You lied to us. To me. At least take some responsibility and admit it."

He winced. "Okay. Yes. I lied in the beginning. I'm sorry. So, so sorry."

His admission didn't make her feel any better. Her anger surged. "It wasn't only in the beginning. If Caitlin hadn't been hurt, you'd still be lying."

He looked at Caitlin but said nothing.

"It was all an act to you, wasn't it? A charade. Playing at being a farmhand. Acting as if you didn't mind having the kids around. Pretending you…" Elisabeth's voice broke. "You were attracted to me."

"No," he said. "Elisabeth, no. Once I got to know you and the kids, everything changed."

"Then why not tell me the truth? Why not get that close to me?"

"Because I was afraid, all right?" The words burst out of him, and he looked almost angry. "I was afraid if you knew Henry Davenport, the real me, you wouldn't want me around anymore."

"Yeah, right."

"It's the truth. My own parents—" His jaw clamped shut.

"Your own parents…what?" she asked softly.

"My own parents knew me better than anyone. And they pretty much decided I was worthless. A disappointment to the mighty Davenport legacy." His eyes darkened. "Maybe I didn't want you to think the same."

"How could I? Henry, you've made such a difference in my life. To the farm. To the kids."

To me.

"Sure, I did." He rolled his eyes. "I screwed up. All the time."

"You tried. All the time. I loved that you tried."

He regarded her somberly. "But could you love me?"

"I…" Fear closed her throat. How could she admit it, knowing what she knew?

"That's what I thought."

She couldn't let him think she hadn't cared about him. Because she did. Or had. "How can I love you? A billionaire? I loved Henry, the farmhand. But—"

"That's who I am." His gaze sought hers. "At least, that's who I want to be."

His words opened Elisabeth's heart and made her want to believe him. But she was scared.

"I'm far from perfect," he explained. "But I don't want to lose you. I'll do whatever it takes to keep you."

"I can't be bought."

"This isn't about money." His sincere tone wrapped around her like a hug. "When I worked on the farm, I finally felt as if I accomplished something. Not with my money, but with my hands. My heart. My soul. It was the second-best feeling in the world."

"The second? What was the first?"

"Kissing you."

A monitor blipped. For a moment, Elisabeth thought it was her heart. She glanced at the bed.

Caitlin's eyes fluttered open, and she looked at Elisabeth. The love in Caitlin's eyes nearly knocked Elisabeth over. Caitlin's gaze rested on Henry. "Daddy?"

The word was so faint, but Elisabeth heard it. A wave of relief, the size of a tsunami, washed over her.

Henry covered Caitlin's hand with his. "I'm right here, princess. And I'm not going anywhere until you can come home with me."

The corners of Caitlin's mouth curved, and she closed her eyes.

A nurse ran into the room. "The monitors showed some movement."

"Caitlin woke up." As Elisabeth backed away from the bed to give the nurse room, tears of joy streamed down her face. "She opened her eyes, spoke, smiled."

The nurse checked Caitlin. "What did she say?"

"Daddy." Henry's voice cracked.

The doctor arrived. Henry and Elisabeth stepped out into the hallway.

"I didn't think she was going to wake up." A sob racked her body. "I really thought we would lose her."

"Not a chance." Henry hugged her. "Caitlin's a fighter. She's strong like her big sister."

The worst seemed to be over, but Elisabeth still struggled to hold it together. Using what little remained of her willpower, she stepped out of Henry's embrace. "Why did you answer when Caitlin called for Daddy?"

"Because she was talking to me," he explained. "She asked if I would be her daddy a couple of weeks ago, but I didn't give her the right answer. I told her I was her *fairy daddy*. Lucky for me, she gave me a second chance today. I wasn't going to blow it this time."

Elisabeth tried to understand what he was saying. "You want to be her daddy?"

"I do." The earnestness of Henry's words brought tears to Elisabeth's eyes. "I told you. I'm not leaving. I want to be Caitlin's daddy and a father figure for Abby and Sam. And for you—"

"I don't need a father figure."

"I was thinking more along the lines of a husband."

Her mouth gaped.

"Okay, this is sudden. We've never been on a date or had a meal without the kids around. But I know it's the right thing to do, and you'll have plenty of time to think about it. You can go back to college and graduate. Maybe attend a music conservatory. Play with an orchestra or two. I'll stay at the farm with the kids until you're ready to come back and get married."

As she stared at him, at Henry, realization dawned. This was no joke. It wasn't a game or an adventure. This was real. He was serious. He wanted to be a permanent fixture at the farm and in her life.

In all their lives.

Her heart swelled with joy.

Henry wasn't going anywhere. He was staying. "You have this all planned out," she said.

"I tend to think I know what's best for…for the people I love," he admitted a bit defensively. "But it's a good plan."

"Are you sure this isn't just you wanting to play fairy godfather? Or plan another adventure?"

"One hundred percent positive."

"You told me you didn't want kids."

"I changed my mind." Hope gleamed in his eyes and matched her own. "Have you changed yours?"

The easiest thing to say was no, but Elisabeth didn't want to do that. She couldn't.

"I have changed my mind. You've given me courage. Not going to lie, I'm still scared, but I choose to push through it," she admitted. "I've been so afraid of being left again I've been relying on excuses to keep my heart safe. My parents, my ex-fiancé, the farm, the kids. It was easier that way. Until I met you."

Henry grinned. "You could have told me."

"Would you have believed me?"

"Probably not."

It was her turn to smile. "Because of you, I opened myself up and became a better person. A better sister."

"You've always been a great sister."

"Thanks." A warm glow flowed through her. "You made me want to live fully, to have fun, to accept help when I needed it, to take a chance on love. But—"

"There can't be a but," he interrupted.

"But you can't plan everything like it's one of your

adventures. You can't tell me what I should do," she explained. "We need to be able to figure things out and make plans together. Okay, Cupid-fairy-godfather Henry?"

He laughed. "You forgot Daddy, and I wouldn't want it any other way."

"Good, because I would like to graduate from college. But playing the harp in an orchestra is an old dream." A surprising peace settled around her heart. "My new dreams revolve around this guy named Henry, who I fell in love with. He seems to think he's a berry farmer."

"I am a berry farmer." Mischief glinted in his eyes. "Or will be, once you say yes."

"Yes?"

"To my marriage proposal." Henry held her hand. "I love you, Elisabeth, and I want you to be my wife. Of course, I'd prefer to wait and propose properly with roses and a horse-drawn carriage and a tasteful yet large diamond ring set in platinum or gold. Your choice."

"I love you, Henry. Not your money. I don't need something fancy or expensive. A plain wedding band is enough."

"I know, but humor me. It'll make life a lot easier for both of us. I also think an engagement harp would be appropriate in addition to a ring."

Elisabeth could barely breathe. She knew enough about Henry to know life would never be boring.

"You're hyperventilating." He squeezed her hand. "I take it that's a good sign?"

All she could do was nod. She didn't need any of those

things he'd mentioned. Sure, they were thoughtful and romantic, but all she needed was Henry. The man she loved.

"Henry Davenport, berry farmer, husband, and father." He grinned. "Kind of catchy, don't you think?"

Epilogue

"Happy birthday, Daddy." Caitlin reached up to give Henry a hug. "I hope you like your party."

"I love my party." It was April Fools' Day—Henry's birthday. The farm-themed party thrown by Sam, Abby, and Caitlin was nothing like the elaborate ones Henry used to throw for himself. This one was a million times better. Just like his life on the berry farm with his wife and the kids. He glanced at Elisabeth, who was passing out pieces of the cake Iris had baked in the shape of a barn to their guests. He kissed the top of Caitlin's head, a mass of short blond ringlets that had grown back since her surgery. "Thank you, princess. And I love the picture you drew for me."

She beamed. "I love you."

With that, she ran off to join Fallon's kids, Audra and Ryder, who were playing with Ruff, and being supervised by

Manny and Frank. Wes, Adam, Kieran, and Brett stood on the porch. Ryland, Mason, and Cade were inside with Sam, probably playing video games. Abby spoke with Paige and Sela, no doubt asking the women a million questions about their careers. Theresa, Brynn, Fallon, Iris, and Dash sat on a blanket in the front yard and played with Noelle and Brecken while Laurel, Cambria, and Rachael talked to Gabe.

Laurel already had lots of ideas for the interior of the house Henry and Elisabeth were having Gabe build. The current farmhouse was crowded enough, and once the baby arrived in November…

Henry grinned. He and Elisabeth were both surprised yet thrilled she'd gotten pregnant during their honeymoon. He loved holidays and thought they should marry on Valentine's Day. They'd had a short engagement, but that was what Elisabeth had wanted. To be honest, he'd been ready to marry her on Thanksgiving or Christmas or New Year's Eve, but he'd been patient, even though that hadn't been easy for him.

The wedding had been an intimate soiree held at the church in Berry Patch, with a reception at a nearby winery. Gabe had escorted the bride down the aisle. Theresa, Abby, and Caitlin had been at Elisabeth's side at the front of the altar. Sam, Brett, and Wes had stood next to Henry. Ruff had been the ring bearer. Adam, Kieran, and Ryland had been ushers. Dash and Mason had been the flower men and put on a show that had people laughing. Everything had been wonderfully and elegantly coordinated by The Posh Planner, a.k.a. Rachael Reese, Mason's wife.

Henry smiled. Family, friends, the farm. He had so much

and wanted everyone to be as happy. He stared at Gabe, who'd caught Elisabeth's bridal garter at their wedding reception. Henry hoped that Gabe and Fallon would connect since all the kids got along so well, but unfortunately, there'd been no spark between them. Still, there had to be a woman out there for Gabriel Logan.

"You seem a million miles away," Elisabeth said.

"I was thinking that Gabe deserves to find the right woman, like I did. He'd be a lot happier. Don't you think?"

"Maybe." Elisabeth smiled. "But your days of sending friends on adventures are over."

"I know," Henry admitted. "I wouldn't have time now to do it anyway. But I wish everyone could experience what we have together."

"You're too sweet." She brushed her lips against his. "But remember, no more matchmaking."

"Cynthia won't let me forget."

"Good for her," Elisabeth teased. "And Gabe."

Henry nodded, but an idea was taking shape in his mind. He couldn't play matchmaker in the way he'd done in the past, but surely, no one would mind if he provided Gabe with an introduction or two...

*****

Thanks for reading *The Payback*. I hope you enjoyed Henry and Elisabeth's story.

If you want to read the next book in the Billionaire Matchmaker series, *The Small Town Adventure,* featuring Gabe Logan, go to melissamcclone.com/billionaire-matchmaker-series.

The Billionaire Matchmaker is a spinoff series from The Billionaires of Silicon Forest. If you'd like to read the *Wedding Lullaby* where Henry sends Laurel and Brett on the tacky wedding adventure mentioned in the book, you can find it at melissamcclone.com/one-night-to-forever. The other books where Henry plays matchmaker with billionaires can be found at melissamcclone.com/billionaires-of-silicon-forest.

Join my newsletter to receive a FREE story and hear about upcoming and new releases, sales, freebies, and giveaways. Just go to melissamcclone.com/subscribe.

I appreciate your help spreading the word. Please tell a friend who loves sweet romance about this book and leave a review on your favorite book site. Reviews help readers find books!

Thanks so much!

About the Author

USA Today bestselling author Melissa McClone has written over sixty sweet contemporary romance and women's fiction novels. She lives in the Pacific Northwest with her husband. She has three young adult children, a spoiled Norwegian Elkhound, and cats who think they rule the house. They do!

If you'd like to find Melissa online:
www.melissamcclone.com
www.facebook.com/melissamcclonebooks
www.facebook.com/groups/McCloneTroopers

Other Books
by Melissa McClone

The Beach Brides/Indigo Bay Miniseries
Prequels to the Berry Lake Cupcake Posse series…
Jenny (Jenny and Dare)
Sweet Holiday Wishes (Lizzy and Mitch)
Sweet Beginnings (Hope and Josh)
Sweet Do-Over (Marley and Von)
Sweet Yuletide (Sheridan and Michael)
Indigo Bay Sweet Romance Collection (Box Set of all five books)

The Berry Lake Cupcake Posse Series
Can five friends save their small town's beloved bakery?
Cupcakes & Crumbs
Tiaras & Teacups
Kittens & Kisses
Wishes & Weddings

Standalone Berry Lake Christmas Book
The Last Cottage on Pinewood Lane

Silver Falls Series
The Andrews siblings find love in a small town in Washington state.
The Christmas Window
A Slice of Summer
A Cup of Autumn
A Sprinkle of Spring

Wedding Bliss
Four friends find love after catching a bridal bouquet.
The Wedding Planner's Secret
The Dress Designer's Promise

One Night to Forever Series
Can one night change your life…and your relationship status?
Fiancé for the Night
The Wedding Lullaby
A Little Bit Engaged
Love on the Slopes
The One Night To Forever Box Set: Books 1-4

The Billionaires of Silicon Forest
Who will be the last single man standing?
The Wife Finder
The Wish Maker
The Deal Breaker
The Gold Digger
The Kiss Catcher
The Game Changer
The Bet Makers (Newsletter exclusive)
The Billionaires of Silicon Forest Prequels
The Billionaires of Silicon Forest Series

Billionaire Matchmaker
A Billionaires of Silicon Forest Spin-off series
featuring Henry Davenport.
The Island Adventure
The Payback Adventure

Mountain Rescue Series
Finding love in Hood Hamlet with a little help
from Christmas magic…
His Christmas Wish
Her Christmas Secret
Her Christmas Kiss
His Second Chance
His Christmas Family

Her Royal Duty
Royal romances with charming princes and dreamy castles...
The Accidental Princess
The Reluctant Princess
The Not-So-Proper Princess
The Proper Princess

Quinn Valley Ranch
Two books featuring siblings in a multi-author series...
Carter's Cowgirl
Summer Serenade
Quinn Valley Ranch Two Book Set

A Keeper at Heart Series
These men know what they want, and love isn't on their list.
But what happens when each meets a keeper?
The Groom
The Soccer Star
The Boss
The Husband
The Date
The Tycoon

For the complete list of books, go to melissamcclone.com/books